Cassie

Cassie

Book Five of the Alpha Series

E. L. Todd

This was the worst date ever.

Tyler kept blabbering about his bowling ball collection. He had every size and every make, storing them in a glass case inside his apartment. He was on a bowling team with his friends from high school and they still kept up the tradition.

I stared at my empty bowl, wishing the waiter would bring the check already. My friend from work, Danielle, set me up with this guy. She clearly had horrible taste in men, or she just hated me. Right now, I wanted to kill her.

"I wax the surface of each ball once a week so it'll keep its shine."

"But you don't use them."

Tyler scratched his head. "They still need to be ready. When they slide across the floor, the friction has to be just perfect."

This guy was the most boring person I'd ever met. I just wanted this night to be over.

"So, do you bowl?"

"No," I said in a bored voice.

"I can teach you," he said.

"No thanks," I said quickly.

He stared at me through his thick glasses. Tyler looked like the typical computer geek. I seriously wondered if he was a virgin. The universe must hate me. I was going to die alone, childless and depressed. I wasn't sure what I did to deserve this but I obviously did something.

"Did you know cashews aren't really a nut?" he asked with a smile.

"What?"

"Cashews. They are actually a seed."

I stared at him blankly.

"I know this because I'm allergic to all nuts but cashews."

I rested my chin on my hand, sighing.

"And did you know they add the smell to gas?" He said this like it was the most interesting thing in the world.

I could be watching the Jimmy Fallon show tonight. But I was stuck with this ridiculously boring guy. And there was absolutely no attraction between us. "I should get going," I said.

He drummed his fingers on the table. "I really like your hair," he blurted.

"Thanks," I said simply.

"It reminds me of mustard."

I raised an eyebrow.

"But in a good way."

The waiter placed the tab on the table before he walked away.

I was so glad to see it. I needed to get the fuck out of there.

Tyler didn't reach for it. "My hair used to be blond but I dyed it brown."

I'd never known a guy that dyed his hair. I glanced at the tab, waiting for him to reach for it. Call me old-fashioned, but the guy should pay for the meal on the first date. And after the social torture I just experienced, I wasn't opening my wallet.

"And I used to be in a band called Dirty Worms."

"I don't even know what to say to that."

He stared at me blankly.

I was irritated that he didn't reach for the check. He was either stalling or just the biggest jerk on the planet. Our conversation didn't flow at all. He just said random things that came to mind. It was like speaking to a person with schizophrenia. Sick of waiting, I grabbed the check.

"What are you doing?" he snapped. He actually showed some sort of emotion.

"Paying the bill."

"Give me that," he yelled. He pulled it from my hands, and the paper and pen fell on the table. His face was red like a tomato. He was seriously pissed. "That was rude."

Now I was getting mad. "You didn't look like you were going to pay."

"You didn't give me a chance."

I kept my mouth shut so this argument would stop immediately. He slid his card inside then left it at the edge of the table. I sighed deeply. Why couldn't he just have cash? Why was this happening to me?

"It's very rude to let a lady pay," he said while he glared at me.

I glared back.

"So, do you want to come back to my place?"

5

Was he being serious? This had to be a joke. "No, thank you."

"I want to show you my bowling collection."

"I'm good."

He stared at me. "I also have a rock collection. I have rocks from every continent."

This guy was the king of the nerds. "I have an early morning tomorrow."

The waiter finally took the tab. I breathed a sigh of relief. This night was almost over.

"And I have a really cool fish tank," he said.

"Interesting," I lied.

"But I don't have any fish yet."

This guy was really weird. I stared at the waiter as he swiped the card through the machine. I was so impatient, my knee was shaking. I just wanted this night to end.

The waiter finally returned.

"Thank god," I whispered.

Tyler looked at me.

"That I didn't spill anything on my dress…"

He stared at me for a second before he slid his card back into his wallet.

We left the restaurant and walked outside.

"It was nice meeting you, Tyler," I said.

"Let me walk you home."

"No," I said quickly. "Our night ends here."

He adjusted his glasses then put his hands in his pockets. He had a gut around the waist and he was short, as tall as I was. He definitely wasn't prince charming. "Well, goodnight." He leaned in to kiss me but I pulled away.

"Bye," I said as I turned around. I didn't look back as I moved through the crowd. After a few blocks, I spotted the sports bar. I seriously needed a drink. That was the worst date I ever had. I knew the baseball game was on so that would calm me down a little. I couldn't believe I missed the game just to go on a date with a total creep. My priorities needed to change.

I walked inside and immediately went to the bar. I sat down then sighed. It was packed with people, mainly guys watching the game.

The bartender looked at me. "You look like you need something strong."

"Scotch."

"That's what I thought."

"On the rocks," I said.

"Coming right up." He made the drink and passed it to me. I downed it in one sitting. I didn't make a face. "Another."

"You got it." He poured it then handed it to me.

I took my time with this one. I sighed and watched the game. The Mariners were playing the Yankees and the game was tied. I was a Yankees fan so I always put my money on them. I would be wearing my jersey instead of this dress if I didn't have a date. After a few minutes, Tyler disappeared from my mind. At least I learned a lot about bowling, not that I ever cared for the sport.

"Bad night?"

I turned and saw Scott smiling at me. "Like you wouldn't believe."

He sat next to me. "Spill it."

"I just had a date from hell."

"Do I need to rip off his head?" he asked seriously.

I laughed. "No. He was just a loser—like all of them."

"I'm sorry," he said sincerely.

I stared at him, admiring his beautiful blue eyes. "Are you sure there are no more single Benedicts?"

He smiled. "Not that I know of."

"Damn…"

"You'll find someone. Don't worry about it."

"That's what everyone keeps telling me," I said.

"Because they are right," he said. "You are smart, beautiful, and amazing. He'll come to you."

"I wish you were a fortune teller."

"Who says I'm not?" He winked at me.

"Where's my girl?"

"She's at home."

"Doing what?"

"She had some work to do. And she doesn't like watching the games with us. She says we're too loud and annoying."

I rolled my eyes. "She's always picked work over pleasure."

"It's a good thing I love her for her tits and that ass," he said with a smile.

"How romantic," I said sarcastically.

"She knows I love her."

"But you love her pussy more than anything."

He shrugged. "Maybe…"

A commercial came on and we turned away from the screen. Scott ordered another beer.

"Can I get you another?" he asked.

"I'm already on my second."

"Scotch?" he asked in a surprised voice. "Are you a middle aged man?"

"On the inside."

"Janet can only handle wine and margaritas."

"She's a lightweight," I said.

"I like it when she's drunk," he said. "The sex is even better."

"You're very open about your relationship."

"Because I know she tells you everything anyway."

I laughed. "She isn't so vulgar about it."

He laughed. "She can be a lady sometimes."

"What's going on over here?" a man said as he patted Scott on the shoulder.

Scott looked at him. "This is my friend Cassie."

He looked at me. His dark brown hair was short but wavy. He had deep green eyes that immediately reminded me of a tropical forest. Something about him looked familiar. I couldn't quite place my finger on it. When he smiled, he had a perfect set of teeth. He was even taller than Scott, over six feet. "It's nice to meet you," he said. "I'm Tony."

I shook his hand. "The pleasure is all mine."

He turned back to Scott. "How do you two know each other?"

"She's Janet's friend."

"My sister has friends?" he asked with a laugh.

I smiled. "She can be very annoying."

Tony looked at me, flashing me another dazzling smile. "I already like her. My sister needs to be put in her place."

"Now I recognize your eyes."

He shrugged. "She and I have some unfortunately similarities."

"Don't worry," I said. "You're clearly the more attractive one."

Tony nodded. "Now I really like you."

"I didn't know Janet had a brother."

"She doesn't mention me often," he said.

Scott eyed us for a moment. He pulled out his phone and looked at it. "I got to make a call." He walked away.

Tony took his seat and looked at the television.

When I watched the game, I caught him staring at me in my peripheral vision.

"You always get dressed up for a sports bar?" he asked.

"No," I said with sigh. "I had a date."

"Oh."

"It didn't go well."

"Oh." He sounded a little happier. "What happened?"

I shrugged. "He talked about his bowling ball collection, something about an empty tank, and how he's allergic to nuts. And not to be shallow, but he wasn't cute at all."

"I think appearances are important when you're looking for a partner. If there's no attraction, the sex will go to shit." He drank from his beer then watched the game. "And he does sound like a freak. You were smart to get out of there."

"Yeah."

"Why did you go out with him to begin with?"

"It was a blind date."

"Yuck," he said. "I don't do blind dates."

"And now I can see why."

He laughed.

I finished my scotch and circled the rim of my glass with my finger.

"You drink scotch?" he asked with a raised eyebrow.

"Only when I'm having a bad day."

"What do you normally drink?"

"I like Long Island Iced Tea."

"You like the strong stuff," he said.

I shrugged. "You like what you like."

"I'm impressed."

I eyed his glass. "Is that light beer?"

He smiled. "When I drink as much as I do, I have to cut back."

"You don't look like you need it." I could tell he was fit and toned under his clothes. There was no way he had a beer belly. If he did, he must be wearing a girdle. I stared at the game and watched the Yankee batter hit the ball out of the park. "Yes!"

Tony yelled at the same time. "That's right!"

I clapped and watched the Yankees get three runs.

Tony eyed me. "You and I are going to get along pretty well."

"Because we like the same team?"

"It's a must for any friendship."

"You must be a sports fanatic."

"You could say that," he said with a smile.

"Who's your favorite football team?"

"The Broncos."

"Really?"

"They have the greatest quarterback in the world."

"Manning?"

"Yep." He drank from his glass again then put it down. "How long have you known my sister?"

"For a few years."

"I wonder why she never mentioned you."

I shrugged. "She probably did but you weren't listening."

"Good point," he said. "I hardly ever listen to my sister."

"That makes two of us."

He chuckled. "Do you like Scott?"

"I   love   him."

"She picked a good one."

"I'm glad she found him. She deserved to find someone special."

"Yeah she did."

I smiled at him.

"I love her—sometimes."

"My brother is the same way. He acts like I'm a pain in his ass but he loves me to death. When my last boyfriend broke up with me, he went postal."

"Why did he break up with you?"

My heart fell. I hated discussing this. "He left me for someone else." I couldn't believe I told him that. It just flew out of my mouth.

"I'm sorry to hear that."

"We were living together so it was hard. I'll never make that same mistake."

"How long ago was this?"

"A while ago," I said vaguely. "I think the Yankees are gonna win." I wanted to change the subject.

"They better," he said. "I got a lot riding on this."

"How much did you bet?"

He took a drink of his beer. "Just some extra change."

We watched the game together. I was surprised he didn't go back and sit with his friends. It was comfortable sitting next to him. Since he was Janet's brother, I knew he was a good guy. I could tell he was just by talking to him. Why wasn't my date been like this? Easy and natural? Why did we have to talk about the scent of gas? I sighed when I thought about it.

"Don't think about it," he said.

"What?"

"Your date."

I smiled. "How'd you know?"

"I can just tell," he said. "Can I buy you another drink?"

"I shouldn't," I said quickly. "I have to walk home, and I don't want to end up in a gutter."

"I'll make sure you get there safely," he said.

I ordered another. "I'm only trusting you because you're Janet's brother."

"That doesn't mean anything," he said with a laugh. "She'll be the first one to tell you that."

"Somehow I doubt it." I drank my scotch and felt my mind buzz. I was glad I took the edge off. My mind was

19

about to collapse on itself. When the game was over, the Yankees were the victors.

Tony danced in place, shaking his hips even though there was no music.

"Nice moves," I said with a laugh.

"You like that?"

I nodded. "Definitely."

"I know what the ladies like."

"I'm sure you do."

Scott approached us and clapped Tony on the shoulder. "Congratulations."

"Thanks," Tony said. "Just don't tell my sister."

"You're lucky I keep your secret." He turned to me. "Can I walk you home, Cassie? I don't mean to be annoying, but I noticed you drank a lot."

"You're so sweet, Scott."

Tony looked at me. "I don't mind walking Cassie. Scott, you should get home to my sister."

Scott looked at me. "Is that okay?"

"Yeah," I said. "We'll be fine."

"Okay," Scott said. "I'll see you later."

"Bye," we both said.

"Are you ready?" Tony asked.

"Yep."

He threw the cash down for both of our drinks.

"I can pay for my own," I said.

"Don't worry about it," he said as he walked out.

When we reached the street I looked at him. "Thank you."

"You're welcome," he said. "So where do you live?"

"A few blocks east."

"Let's go."

We walked side by side down the sidewalk. Tony had his hands in his jeans.

"Where do you work?" he asked.

21

"Castle magazine."

"What do you do?"

"I'm a fashion designer."

"Cool," he said.

I rolled my eyes. "I know you think it's lame."

He smiled. "I don't think that at all."

"I like it a lot," I said. "It's always something I've been interested in."

"I think you should do what you love. Not doing it would be stupid."

"And what do you do?"

"I'm a sports analyst."

"And what is that?"

"I advise people on sporting events and teams."

"I still don't understand what that is," I said honestly.

"It's complicated..."

We arrived at my building and took the stairs to my floor. When I walked up, I wondered if he was looking at me ass. I wanted to check but I didn't want to make it obvious. When we reached my apartment, my heart fell. Tyler was leaning against my door. I stopped immediately.

"What's wrong?" Tony asked.

"Uh, nothing."

He stared at me. "I can see it in your eyes."

I nodded down the hallway. "That's the guy I had the date with."

Tony looked. "Why is he here?"

"I don't fucking know," I whispered. I crossed my arms over my chest. I never had a guy just show up to my place like that. A part of me was scared. This guy was so weird. Imagine what he had in mind.

Tony looked into my eyes, seeing the fear. "I'll take care of him."

"No," I said quickly. "Don't worry about it. I'm fine, really."

Tony walked toward Tyler.

I sighed and waited.

Tony stopped and looked at him. "What the fuck are you doing?"

Tyler flinched at the hostility. "I'm waiting for someone..."

"My girlfriend lives here."

"Your girlfriend?" he asked.

Tony's eyes widened in anger. "Are you stalking my girlfriend?"

"No, I'm waiting for Cassie."

"That's my girlfriend," he snapped.

"Oh…"

"Now get the fuck away from here. If I ever see you again, I'll beat the fucking shit out of you." He pushed him against the wall, making his glasses fall on the ground.

Tyler looked scared. "I'm sorry…"

"You should be, fucking asshole." He put his foot over the glasses.

"Please don't," Tyler said. "I'm practically blind without them."

"You'll be literally blind if I ever see your face again."

"Okay," he whispered.

Tony stepped back and let Tyler get away. He walked down the hallway and took the stairs at the end. I breathed a sigh of relief when he was gone.

Tony came back to me. "He won't bother you again."

"Thank you," I said.

He smiled. "You're welcome."

"I'm not a coward," I said. "I just panicked for a second."

"I didn't think you were," he said. "I know it can be scary for a single girl in the city."

I walked to my door and he followed behind me. I grabbed my keys from my purse and held them in my grasp. I felt awkward for a moment, unsure what to do. When I looked at Tony, I saw the green eyes that I immediately felt drawn to. He was a sweet guy, cool and easy to get along with. And he was so good-looking and charming. I can't believe Janet never mentioned him before.

"Cassie, I think you're really cool," Tony said. "I would love to take you out sometime."

My heart fluttered.

Tony stared at me. "Are you free tomorrow?"

"Uh…"

He cringed. "I got rejected just like your date."

"No," I said quickly. "I just—you're my best friend's brother."

"So?"

"Well, I have to talk to her first."

He sighed. "It's just a date. I didn't ask you to marry me."

"But it's still rude not to mention it."

"How about we go on a date first then go from there. There's no point in asking her permission if you don't even like me. Who knows? I might be as weird as that guy I just chased off."

I laughed. "I find that very unlikely."

He shrugged. "You never know. Who cares about my sister?"

"Okay," I said with a smile.

"Great," he said. "I'll pick you up tomorrow at six. Is that good?"

I nodded.

"And you like hockey, right?"

"I love hockey."

"You're already the perfect woman," he said. "Make sure you wear something warm."

"Are you taking me to a game?"

"It's a surprise." He winked.

"I guess you could be taking me skiing…"

He laughed. "I'll see you then."

"Okay."

Tony turned away. "Goodnight."

"Tony?"

"Yeah?"

"Thank you for walking me home and taking out the trash."

He smiled. "Anytime, Cassie."

2

At work the next morning, I was arranging the dresses in the fitting room when Orlando walked in.

"Her Majesty is coming," he said with a smile. He kept his back straight as he walked and smiled brightly, showing his dazzling teeth. His vest was tight around his torso and his slacks were thin. "You ready for this, girl?" he said as he waved his hand.

I smiled. "I'm as ready as I'll ever be."

Orland kissed me on the cheek. "You'll be fine, babe."

"I hope so." I checked the seams on the dress and returned it to the rack. "How was your night?"

Orlando smiled. "Steward and I went out to dinner."

"That sounds nice."

"It was really nice when we got home."

I laughed. "I bet it was." Orland was one of the many gay men that worked for the magazine. He and I just clicked immediately. Whenever I saw him at work, my day was better. He was the best girlfriend ever, only he was a boy. He gave me a lot of great tips that I incorporated into my work.

"So how'd that date go?"

I rolled my eyes. "You don't even want to know."

He hopped on his toes. "Spill it, lady."

"He was a total weirdo."

Orland cringed. "That bad?"

"I couldn't get out of there fast enough. And when I got home, he was waiting by my door. Thankfully, Tony took care of it."

"Who's Tony?"

"Oh," I said. "My friend's brother. He walked me home."

Orlando smiled. "What's he like?"

I blushed. "He's very sweet."

"Maybe you should go out with him instead."

"Actually, we are going out tonight."

He clapped. "Something good always comes out of bad situations."

"I suppose," I said with a sigh.

"Why the long face?" he asked.

"Well, it's my best friend's brother."

"Your point?"

"I feel guilty not telling her."

"Don't," he said. "Test out the car before you buy it. Let him buy you dinner then test out his skills in the bedroom. If he sucks, you don't have to tell her about it at all."

I shook my head. "I'm not sleeping with him on the first date."

He shrugged. "It would save you a lot of time."

"We're going to a hockey game."

"Wow," Orlando said. "This guy is super straight."

I laughed. "I guess you could say that."

"But that's not very romantic," he said as he shook his head.

"I like hockey," I said. "I don't mind. And I don't want it to be too serious anyway. It's just more relaxing this way."

"Then take him back to your place and do the deed."

"Orlando!"

"What?" he said with a smile. "I slept with Steward on the first date and now we live together."

"And you slept with ten other guys on the first date before you found him."

"Imagine how much time I would have wasted if I didn't speed up the process," he said with a wink.

I shook my head then arranged the dressed on the rack.

Gloria came into the room. "What am I wearing?" She was standing in her underwear and bra, not self-conscious about being half naked. All the models were used to the exposure.

"Here," I said as I handed it to her. "The heels are in the dressing room."

"Thanks." She walked inside the changing room. Her body was so thin. Her ribs were noticeable on her sides, and her arms were thin and lanky. I knew I was fairly petite but I wasn't even that small. But I liked the way my body was. And I loved food.

Orlando stared at me. "Maybe you should hit the runway."

"What?"

"You're such a pretty girl," he said as he lifted my chin.

I rolled my eyes. "I belong behind the curtain. I love eating chili dogs and French fries way too much."

"And you still look great," he said. "Maybe you should think about it."

"I'll stick to designing."

"Whatever," he said.

Winnie came in and grabbed the other dress. "This is nice," she said as she looked at it.

"Thank you."

She walked into the changing room while Orlando and I waited.

The two girls came out and appraised themselves in the mirror. I walked over with my tape measurer and my pins. The fabric clung to their bodies perfectly. Nothing seemed out of place. My work was done.

Pia, the chief editor of the magazine, came inside with her assistant behind her. She wore a black dress with designer heels. A scarf was around her neck and she wore dangling earrings. Her face was stoic and hard to decipher. No one ever knew what she was thinking. I held my breath as she walked inside. She didn't look at me once.

Pia came to Gloria and examined the dress. She walked completely around her, feeling the fabric in her fingers and testing the quality of the zipper. Then she moved to Winnie and did the same thing. She pulled her glasses off and thought for a long moment. Orlando kept glancing at me, waiting for the verdict.

"No."

My heart fell. "No?"

Pia shook her head. "Just no."

I took a deep breath, remaining calm. "What changes would you like me to make?"

"Make something that isn't hideous," she snapped. She stormed out while her assistant followed close behind her.

"Yikes," Gloria said.

"We're so sorry," Winnie said.

"It's not your fault," I said.

Orlando patted my shoulder. "You'll get it right next time."

I sighed. "She doesn't give me any feedback. I can't read her mind."

"Nobody can, babe," Orlando said.

Gloria looked at herself in the mirror. "Well, I really like it."

"You can keep it," I said. "I'm obviously not going to be using it."

The models walked back into the changing rooms and pulled off the dresses. They handed them to me before they left.

I kept my emotions under the surface but they were raging. I was hurt. I worked so many hours on these gowns and Pia pretty much spit on them. It was always a hit and miss with her. And when she did like my work, I received no praise, just a simple nod. I felt unappreciated and undervalued.

Orlando caught the look. "Don't let it get you down."

"I'm just frustrated. I know I'm a good designer. If I had my own business, I know I would flourish."

"Then do it," he said.

I shook my head. "I don't have the money to start it up. I'm stuck here."

"You can't save your money?"

"I barely make it by as it is."

"I'm sorry, dear."

"Yeah..."

"At least you have a date tonight with a hot guy."

I sighed. "That's true."

"Do you think that other guy is gay?" he asked.

"I don't know...I didn't think about it."

"That might explain why he's so odd. He feels out of place and he's trying to blend in. Who is he?"

"His name is Tyler. He works for IT."

He nodded. "Maybe I can help."

I laughed. "You're going to take him out of the closet?"

"Girl, I'm going to push him out of it."

I smiled. "You're very controlling, Orlando."

"Steward says he likes it."

"I bet." I pushed the cart against the wall then gathered my supplies. Now I had to start over but I had no ideas. Creativity didn't just fall out of my head. It would take me some time. But Pia didn't understand that. I loved my job but I hated working here. But there was no way around it.

"Stop it," Orland said.

"What?"

"You keep pitying yourself."

"So?"

"Don't," he said. "Change it."

"Okay," I said. "I just need to start brainstorming."

"Get laid tonight. It will help."

"I'm sure Tony would love that," I said with a laugh.

"He'll want to help you out in whatever way he can."

"What a good friend," I said sarcastically.

3

Since we were going to a hockey game, I decided to dress casual. I wore a long sleeve shirt with a nice jacket and jeans. It was always cold in the arena because of the ice, and I would rather dress warm than look cute. The game would last about two hours.

A six o' clock sharp, Tony knocked on the door.

I smiled at his punctuality. When I opened it, he was smiling at me. The green color of his eyes looked brighter than last time. He wore a gray hoodie and dark jeans. Even though he looked casual, he looked very attractive. The broadness of his shoulders was evident in anything he wore. He had long legs that were toned and firm. The longer I stared at him, the more I realized I was being a pervert by gawking at him.

"Cassie?"

"Huh?"

"I said hi."

"Oh," I said. "Hey."

"You look nice."

"Thank you." I kept staring at him.

He put his hands in his pockets and said nothing. After a moment, he spoke. "So…are you ready to go?"

"Oh yeah," I said, shaking my head. I sounded like such an idiot right now.

"Are you okay?" he asked.

"Yeah," I said. "I just didn't know that Janet had a hot brother."

A smile appeared on his face and his cheeks tinted. "Thanks."

Why did I just say that? "I'm sorry. Sometimes I speak without thinking."

"And I'm glad you did," he said. "And I'm equally confused. I'm not sure why my sister never mentioned you. So far, you sound pretty damn perfect."

"Wait until you get to know me better," I said with a laugh.

"I plan to."

I grabbed my purse then locked my apartment door. We left the building and walked outside until we reached the cab. Tony kept his hands in his pockets and didn't touch me, but he did open the door for me.

When we sat in the backseat, I kept thinking about his hands. They were resting in his lap, nowhere near mine. I wanted him to touch me, which was odd. I usually hated it when guys were affectionate on the first date. But it didn't feel like a first date. It seemed like we were hanging out at as friends, but it also felt like we had already dated, like this was our tenth or twelfth date. I couldn't explain it.

"How are you?" he asked.

"Good. How about you?"

"Has that guy bothered you?" he said quickly.

"Tyler?"

"Whatever that freak's name is." The anger escaped his voice. It happened so suddenly.

"No, he hasn't bothered me."

"Good," he said. "I'm glad I don't have to kill anyone today."

"Or ever."

He smiled. "You never know. So how was work?"

I shrugged. "It was okay."

"It sounds like it was less than okay."

"I finished the gowns I was showcasing but my boss rejected them. Now I have to start all over."

"What was wrong with them?" he asked.

"I don't know. She didn't give me any feedback."

"That's odd…"

"It's frustrating."

He smiled at me. "Well, you are going to forget about all of that at the game. I'll make sure you have a good time."

"Okay," I said. "As long as you get me a chili dog."

He stared at me. "Seriously, why didn't Janet mention you? You're, like, totally awesome."

I laughed. "Janet definitely doesn't think I'm awesome. In fact, she'll tell you I'm a thorn in her backside."

He shook his head. "That brat."

"She is a brat."

He gave me a high-five. "Now you are even better. I love picking on my sister with people."

"We can't gang up on her."

Tony cringed. "Damn, you were so close to being my soul mate."

I laughed. "Well, Janet and Layla are my soul mates. I'm already taken."

"There's room for more, right?"

"Maybe."

We arrived at the game and came to the line. It was huge, wrapping all the way around the building. The game was about to start so I knew we would probably miss the first half.

"This way," Tony said as he went around.

"What are you doing?"

"Come on," he said.

I followed him until we reached separate doors.

"Hello, Mr. Hannigan."

"Hello, Nate."

He took the tickets and scanned them. "Enjoy the show." He opened the doors for us and allowed us to walk inside.

"What was that?" I asked.

"What?"

"How did you cut through the line?"

"Oh," he said. "I have special tickets."

That surprised me.

The inside was crowded with people so Tony placed his arm around my waist. As soon as he touched me, I flinched, not expecting him to do that. The sensation was brief and weak, my thick jacket blocking most of the affection, but it still sent shivers down my spine. I liked the touch.

He guided me toward the seats, and we moved until we reached the very first row, right in the center of the game. The glass was right in front of us and the players were just a few feet away. I'd never had better seats at any game.

"How did you get these seats?' I asked.

He shrugged. "I know a guy."

We sat down and he leaned back. "What would you like to eat?"

"I can get it," I said quickly.

He smiled. "Cassie, tell me what you want, please."

He was bossy but sweet at the same time. It was hard to dislike it. "Chili dog with onions, nachos, and a soda."

Tony nodded. "That's impressive."

"You'll be even more impressed when you watch me eat it all."

"Do you want a beer?"

"Oh yeah! A beer too," I said with a laugh. "But I'll come with you. There's no way you can carry all of that."

Tony shook his head and raised his hand.

A man wearing a slacks and a collared shirt approached us out of thin air. "Good evening, Mr. Hannigan. What can I get you?"

Tony smiled at him. "My date will have a chili dog with onions, nachos, a Pepsi, and a beer. I'll have the same." He opened his wallet and forked over the cash.

He nodded. "I'll be back."

"Thank you," Tony said.

I stared at him incredulously. "What was that?"

"What?"

"You have a servant?"

He laughed. "He isn't a servant. He just works here."

"Does he do that for everyone?"

"No."

The game started and Tony started clapping. "Let's get this game going."

I stared him suspiciously. Something wasn't adding up.

"Tony!"

Tony turned to a man standing next to him. "Hey, Mike. What's up?"

"You're betting on the Rangers?"

"Of course," Tony said. "They got the best team in the league right now."

"How much you got riding on it?"

"Fifty dimes."

Mike whistled. "Good luck to you."

"I don't need the luck, but thanks."

Mike looked at me. "And who's this?"

"My apologies," Tony said. "This is my date, Cassie."

"It's nice to meet you."

"You too," I said politely.

"She's cute," Mike said. "What's she doing with you?"

"I think she's lost," Tony said.

Mike laughed. "Keep her lost for your sake."

Tony nodded. "I will."

Mike walked away and joined a group of guys in a different row.

"You're very popular," I said.

Tony shrugged. "I have a lot of friends who are obsessed with sports."

"What's a dime?"

Tony jumped up and clapped when the Rangers scored. "Yes!"

I clapped and whistled.

When he sat down, he pulled his sweater off, revealing his jersey. His body was more prominent under the thin material. I could see the outline of his chest. It was chiseled and hard. Tony turned to me and placed the jacket around my shoulders.

"Aren't you cold?" I asked.

"No, I'm always hot."

Literally. "Okay."

The man returned with all the food. I immediately dug in while Tony tipped him.

"Thank you, sir."

Tony nodded.

I glanced at his hand and saw the hundred dollar bill. Was he rich? Or was he famous or something?

Tony drank his beer and watched the game intently. I ate all my food then finished off my beer.

Tony stared at me. "Wow."

"What?"

"You ate everything?"

I smiled. "I wasn't kidding."

"That's—hot."

I laughed. "You have an odd definition of the word." I turned back to the game and cheered when the Rangers scored.

Tony stared at me. "You like hockey?"

"I've been to a few games with my brother."

"Do you have a favorite team?"

"No," I said. "But I like to watch."

He nodded. "You're perfect."

"You said that already."

"I just have to make it clear." He turned back to the game and watched the Ranger score.

When he wasn't looking, I smelled his jacket. I liked the scent. It was manly. He and I had a great time watching the game. We both screamed hysterically when the ref called a foul on the Rangers. And I drank two more beers, which made Tony smile. The date was comfortable and easy. I had the nerves but I felt calm at the same time. And I kept wondering why Tony had all these connections. It was odd. He said he was a sports analyst. How much did people like that get paid?

When the game ended, the Ranger won.

"Yes!" Tony said. "That was awesome."

"Thanks for taking me along."

He smiled at me. "Did you have fun?"

"I had a lot of fun. I'm surprised Janet doesn't bug you to take her."

He shook his head. "I only take people I like."

I laughed. "You act like you hate her."

"I don't," he said. "I just prefer spending time with her boyfriend."

"You love her."

He shrugged. "I might." He stood up and pulled me to stand. He didn't take his jacket back, which I was grateful for. I wasn't cold, but I loved the smell of it. We left the stadium, bypassing the crowd by taking a different exit. None of the security officers stopped him or even questioned him. It was like everyone knew exactly who he was.

We took a cab back to my place, and he walked me to the door.

"I had a really great time with you," he said. "A *really* great time."

"I did too."

He didn't lean in to kiss me. Tony didn't even touch me.

I kept waiting.

"Can I take you to dinner on Thursday?"

"Yeah," I said immediately.

"So, was I a freak like that other guy?"

"Not at all," I said with a smile.

"Good."

"If we go out again, I should probably talk to Janet."

"Why? It's none of her business who I date."

I sighed. "She's my best friend. She deserves to know."

He rolled his eyes. "Women are so weird."

"Don't you think it's odd that she never introduced us before? We totally get along. Why would she have hid that? There has to be a reason."

Tony was quiet for a moment. "I have no idea what that reason would be."

"Maybe she doesn't want her friends to date her brother."

"That's too damn bad."

"Well, she's my best friend. I can't piss her off."

"I'm her family and I have no problem doing that."

I laughed. "Because she has to love you."

"I guess that explains why she still talks to me."

I grabbed my keys and held them in my hand. "Would you like to come inside?"

His eyes shined a little brighter. "I would love to."

I opened the door and he followed behind me.

"Can I make you some coffee?"

"Sure."

"How do you take it?"

"Black."

"Okay."

I made it for him then brought it to the living room. He sat down and took a sip.

"That's good."

"It's Ethiopian."

"I'll have to get some."

"I found it at the farmers market."

Tony nodded. "I'll have to stop by."

I took off his jacket and mine.

He glanced at my body for a moment before he looked away. "You have a nice apartment."

"Thank you."

"Do you live alone?"

"Yeah."

"I live alone too."

I turned toward him and stared at his face. His fair skin was bright and beautiful. He had a good complexion for a guy. He didn't seem scarred and rugged like most other men. His chin was hairless but I could see the faint growth underneath. Through the cut of his jersey I could see that he didn't have any chest hair, which I preferred. Now I wondered what the rest of him looked like.

"What are you thinking?" he asked.

"Huh?"

"What are you thinking?" he repeated.

"About the game," I lied.

"You seemed pretty lost in thought."

"I'm pretty serious about sports."

"My kind of woman."

"So…"

"So…?"

The tension hung in the air. I wanted to say something but I couldn't think of anything. I suddenly became very nervous. I wasn't sure why. He stared at me and I waited for something to happen, for him to kiss me, but it never came to pass.

"Where did you go to college?" he asked.

"NYU."

He nodded. "Good school."

"My parents weren't happy when I decided to major in art fashion."

"Fuck them," he said bluntly.

I smiled. "You don't care what other people think, do you?"

"Never."

"Well, they paid for my education so I understood their objection."

"That still doesn't matter," he said. "Now you work for a fashion magazine and you can afford this apartment on that salary. Obviously, you didn't make a mistake. You are a successful young woman. They should be proud."

"I wish they felt the same."

"Well, I'm proud of you," he said. "Tell them that."

"I think I will."

He rested his hand on his thigh.

I watched it for a moment, wondering how it would feel to squeeze it.

"Well, thank you for the wonderful evening," he said. "I should probably go."

"Oh," I said sadly.

He caught the look. "Unless you want me to stay…"

"I would love it if you stayed, but you can go if you want."

"I just didn't want to overstay my welcome."

"You didn't," I said quickly.

"Cool," he said with a nod. He stayed on his side of the couch.

I never wanted to be kissed more in my life. Most of the time, I had the opposite problem. I wanted the freaks to get away from me. I wanted Tony to kiss me, slip his tongue inside my mouth. I could tell just by looking at him that he would be a good kisser. Then I imagined what he would be like in bed…I stopped the thought. I hadn't gotten in laid in over a year. I was going through the worst dry spell ever. I really liked Tony and thought he was a sweet guy. I wanted to take this slow but I also wanted to jump his bones.

He grabbed the remote and turned on the TV. "Let's see if there's anything good on."

I sighed in frustration. I moved closer to him on the couch and sat right beside him.

He picked a channel with a college game on. We watched it together and shouted when his team scored. He didn't grab my hand. Maybe he didn't kiss me because he thought I didn't want to be kissed. I turned toward him so my face was near his. If that wasn't a clear signal, I didn't know what was.

He still didn't take the bait. He leaned back and drank from his coffee. When it got really late, he turned off the TV. "I should get going."

"Yeah," I said. "I have work."

He stood up and grabbed his sweatshirt, pulling it over his head. It messed up his hair but it still looked sexy. I walked him to the door and leaned closer to him.

"I can't wait to see you on Thursday."

"Me too," I whispered. I stared into his face, waiting for him to embrace me or kiss me. *Something.*

He opened the door and walked out. "Goodnight."

I closed the door, sighing in frustration.

4

"He didn't even kiss you?" Orlando said when we had lunch.

"Nope," I said in annoyance.

"Okay, he has to be gay."

"You think everyone is gay."

"And I'm always right."

"I know he isn't gay," I said. "But I don't know why he didn't do anything."

"Did you make it clear you wanted to be kissed?"

"*Very* clear," I said. "I'm so annoyed."

"Did he at least hug you?"

"Nope."

"Is he Mormon?"

I laughed. "I don't think so."

"Why didn't you just kiss him?"

"I wasn't sure if he wanted me to," I said. "I mean, if I was making it clear I wanted to be kissed, why didn't he take the shot? He obviously didn't want to."

"I'm sure there's a reason." Orlando sprinkled the sugar into his coffee then sipped it.

"Maybe he isn't attracted to me."

"Shut up!" Orlando rolled his eyes. "I may be gay but I can guarantee that isn't why."

"Then what?"

"Maybe he's old-fashioned."

"He doesn't seem like it. And I think he's rich or famous."

"Why?"

"People were treating him like he was VIP at the game. And they were talking about betting dimes or something."

"Dimes?" Orland asked.

I took a bite of my sandwich then wiped my mouth with a napkin. "He said he bet fifty dimes. Like fifty cents?"

Orlando's eyed widened. "In betting, a dime is a grand."

I dropped my sandwich. "So he meant fifty grand?"

Orlando nodded. "You got yourself a sugar daddy."

My mind was racing. "So he is rich?"

"He must be. That's the only explanation."

"I guess that makes sense. If he is rich, he's very humble about it."

"This guy sounds like a catch," Orlando said. "Are you sure he isn't gay?"

I glared at him. "What about Stewart?"

He rolled his eyes. "He'd understand. He would leave me for Anderson Cooper any day."

"But that guy is old," I said.

"He doesn't care. Cooper is on his list."

I laughed. "You guys are funny."

"We have an odd relationship."

I finished my sandwich while I thought about Tony. I still couldn't figure out why he was so distant with me. I guess I could just ask him next time I see him. And I wondered why Janet had never introduced me to him. He and I hit it off immediately. Tony was sweet, successful, funny, and gorgeous. Why would she hide him? Then it hit me.

"Janet didn't tell me about him because of his money," I said.

"What?"

"My best friend kept her brother a secret because she probably assumed I'd only date him for his cash."

Orlando shook his head. "That doesn't sound like something you'd do."

"I know it isn't." I sighed sadly. "I'm hurt she would ever think that."

"Don't jump to conclusions," Orlando said. "You have no idea. Maybe it's the other way around. Maybe she didn't think Tony was good enough or you."

"I highly doubt that," I said. "He's the perfect guy. I haven't had a date go that well in my entire life. Orlando, he's so sexy. You have no idea."

"I wish I had an idea."

I laughed. "I'll try to snap a picture."

"If you guys get serious, we should double date."

"That's an idea," I said. "But I don't want you and Stewart fighting over him."

Orlando rolled his eyes. "He's straight. We get it. Don't get all jealous on me."

I smiled. "Sorry."

We left the café and went back to work. When we walked into the office, Charli, the receptionist approached me. She was carrying a large vase with dark red roses. It was huge, almost too heavy for her to carry.

"These are for you," she said.

I took them from her, almost dropping them on the floor. "Are you sure?"

"It says Cassie on the card."

"Thank you."

Orlando smiled at me. "Let's go in your office."

We went into the studio and I put them on the table. Orlando clapped his hands while he watched me open the card.

"What does it say?" he said excitedly.

I read it aloud.

Cassie,

I had a wonderful time with you the other night. I've never met such a cool chick that loves sports, beer, and food as much as I do. You're my dream girl. And I'm sorry I didn't kiss you. I won't make the same mistake on Thursday.

P. S. I hope this will hold you over.

A chocolate kiss was sitting inside.

Orlando practically screamed. "That is so cute!"

I stared at the letter again, my heart racing. "The flowers are beautiful."

"I told you he wanted to kiss you."

"I guess you were right."

Orland hopped on his toes. "He sounds so dreamy."

"He is pretty amazing."

"I'm so jealous," he said. "Stewart and I used to be that way. Now we fart and burb in front of each other."

I laughed. "That's pretty romantic."

He sighed. "I know."

"But I'm jealous of you."

"How do you mean?"

"You're with someone that still loves to be around you all the time. Even if that heat isn't as strong, that love is even stronger."

He smiled. "You do have a point."

I smelled a rose and sighed. Now I couldn't wait until Thursday.

5

Since Janet had become serious with Scott, they started running together every morning. Therefore, our gym sessions were over. But I didn't mind. I knew she was happy with Scott so I was happy for her. And she said they had morning sex in the shower after every run, so I definitely couldn't hold that against her. I missed having sex. I couldn't even remember what it felt like anymore. Had it changed since I was last in the game?

When I thought about Tony, the idea of sex wasn't far behind. Having sex with him seemed like it would be easy and enjoyable. I couldn't explain why, but I was innately comfortable around him. I liked him as a person, and I liked him as someone in the bedroom. That was a first for me. I never liked someone's personality and was insanely attracted to them at the same time. It was usually one or the other. Perhaps that was why my last boyfriend left me. I didn't like thinking about it. I pushed the thought away.

When Tony knocked on my door, my heart exploded. I was nervous. I checked my hair in the mirror one more time before I answered the door. Since we were going to dinner, I put on a nice dress that complemented my skin tone. It highlighted the right curves in the right places. I really wanted him to kiss me so I was putting all my cards on the table.

I opened the door and smiled.

He stared at my face then his gaze moved to my body. Tony blatantly checked me out, taking in my every curve. I felt the heat from his eyes as they drilled into me. I tried to think of something to say but I was at a loss for words. He wore a t-shirt and jeans, and he looked sexy like he always did. I couldn't believe he was Janet's brother. He was too hot to be related to her.

Tony stepped inside and shut the door behind me. Without speaking, he came to me then placed his hands on my waist, feeling the fabric of my dress. My heart was racing so fast, I thought it would give out. When he pressed his face close to mine, I breathed heavily. I waited for it, knowing it was coming.

He cupped my face and pressed his lips against mine. I took a deep breath when I felt his soft lips. He parted mine then kissed me softly, his mouth breathing into me. I knew he was a good kisser but I wasn't expecting this. I actually felt my knees go weak. Tony rubbed his nose against mine for a moment, looking at me. Then he returned to kissing me. No tongue was involved but it was still sensual, loving. I felt a quiet sigh escape my lips. I missed being touched like this. I had been dormant for so long, and now my hibernation had ended. The heat surged back into me. I placed my hands on his chest and felt the solid wall underneath this shirt. I moaned again as I kissed him. I was insanely attracted to him. The area between my legs burned.

Tony broke the kiss then stared at me. "You're a good kisser," he whispered.

"You're even better."

"I liked hearing you moan."

My cheeks blushed.

"Maybe I shouldn't have done that before dinner."

"Why?" My hands were still on his chest.

"Now I don't want dinner." His hands touched my waist, his fingers rubbing into my muscles. "You're so small."

"Thanks."

"You're perfect."

"I'm far from perfect. I have too many flaws to count."

"Maybe all the flaws make you perfect. I like real women, humble women."

I stared at his lips, wanting him to kiss me again.

"One more," he whispered. He leaned in and pressed his mouth against mine. I immediately dug my fingers into his hair, wanting to savor the moment before it ended. The heat flushed through my body and the frostbite melted. Now I was only hungry for dessert.

Tony pulled away. "Are you ready?"

I nodded.

"Then let's go."

I sighed, wishing we would stay here.

We left the apartment and went to a small Italian restaurant. Tony grabbed my hand and held it while we walked. It was a nice change from our first date. I liked the affection he was giving me. It felt right.

When we arrived at our table, he pulled out the chair for me before he sat across from me. He picked up his menu and browsed the selections.

I took advantage of the opportunity to stare at him.

When he looked up, I looked down.

"You look beautiful tonight," he said. "I forgot to say that earlier when I was thinking it."

"I think you said it non-verbally."

He smiled. "I'm glad you picked up on that. So what are you getting?"

"Tortellini," I said.

"Good choice," he said. "I think I'll be having a pizza."

When I looked at the prices next to the menu, my eyes widened. This place was ridiculously expensive. I couldn't believe we were eating there. The progression of our dates was a little odd. First, we went to a hockey game, and now we were having a romantic dinner. I didn't question it.

"How was work today?" he asked.

"Thank you for the flowers. They were beautiful."

He smiled. "You're welcome."

"My friend Orlando was jealous."

"Why?"

"He wishes his boyfriend would send him flowers like that."

"They were lovely," he said.

"So, why didn't you kiss me the other night?"

He stared at the menu again. "It just wasn't the right time."

I didn't know what that meant. "Because it was our first date?"

"Yeah," he said vaguely.

I decided to drop it. "So, did you bet fifty grand on that Rangers game?"

He met my gaze. "Why do ask that?"

"You told Mike you bet fifty dimes."

"Oh," he said. "I didn't know you heard that."

I waited for him to answer my question but he never did. I was starting to realize how secretive he was. I decided to discuss something else. "Where do you live?"

He drank from his water then returned it to the table. The candle in the center flickered for a moment. "A few blocks from Janet."

"Isn't that too close?" I teased.

"I keep the dead bolt on."

"Are you good friends with Scott?"

"Yeah, Janet says the two of us are joined at the hip."

"That's cute."

"He's a cool guy. We have a good time together."

I nodded. "I'm sure that makes Janet happy."

"And I can keep him an eye on him."

"I thought you didn't like your sister?" I said with a smile.

"Damn…you caught me."

"I knew you loved her."

"So, where does your brother live?"

"In the city," I said. "He's a sports agent."

"Really?" he asked with interest.

"He says he loves it."

"Wow. That's awesome. He and I would have a lot to talk about."

I nodded. "You would."

"Are you close with your parents?"

"My dad, not really my mom."

"Why is that?' he asked.

"My dad and I just get along better. I was a tomboy growing up."

He smiled. "That makes sense."

"My mom always tried to get me to do cheerleading or ballet, but I wanted to play basketball with my dad and brother, getting dirty and smelly."

"If I had a daughter, I would love it if she was that way."

"I can't see you having a daughter," I said. "You seem like you'd prefer a son."

He shrugged. "I'd be happy with either."

"Do you want to have kids?"

"I don't know. I think I'd be happy either way."

I nodded. "I don't mean to ask something personal, but how old are you?"

"Twenty six."

"Oh. You're only a year older than me."

"Yep. My sister and I too close in age. I think that's why she and I get along so well. When we were younger, I'd prefer to hang out with my sister over my friends any day. As much as I hate to admit it, she's pretty cool."

I smiled. "That's sweet."

"Don't tell her I said that."

"I'm sure she already knows."

"Yeah, she's a little conceited brat."

I laughed. "She's the most humble person I know."

"I disagree," he said. "You're the hottest chick I've ever seen but you don't act like it."

I blushed at his comment. I wasn't expecting that. "I don't know about that..."

"When I saw you in that bar, I was immediately smitten. And when I saw Scott talking to you, I knew I was in. I just swooped."

I looked at my menu because I didn't know what else to do.

"I'm sorry if my bluntness offended you."

"It didn't," I said quietly.

The waiter took our orders then walked away. Tony ordered a bottle of wine for us and we drank it together. It was red wine with an equal amount of sweetness and tartness.

"So, are you equally fond of Beatriz?" I asked. "Because I want to punch her in the face most of the time."

Tony laughed loudly. "That deserves another high-five." He clapped my hand loudly. "I was never close with her like I was with Janet, but I still love her unconditionally. I'm glad she worked things out with Hank, especially for my nephew."

"Do you like being an uncle?"

"I love it," he said. "I want more so I can have my own baseball team."

I laughed. "Janet and Scott need to get started then."

He grimaced.

"Sorry, I guess that was a bad mental picture."

"It's okay," he said. "Can I ask you something personal?"

My heart raced. "I guess."

"You don't have to answer it if you don't want to."

"Okay."

"You said you were in a relationship that ended like two years ago. Do you still talk to him?"

"No."

He nodded. "Was he cheating on you the entire time?"

"I never asked. At that point, it didn't matter."

Tony stared at me. "Have you been in a relationship since then?"

"No."

"Have you dated?"

"Yeah," I said. "But they were all losers and never went anywhere."

He gripped his knife and held it in his hand.

"Those weren't that personal."

"Well, the last one is the most personal. I feel bad for even asking."

"What is it?" I swallowed the lump in my throat.

"Have you…had sex since then?"

My cheeks blushed. "No…"

Tony nodded.

"Why do you ask?"

"You just seem…"

"Charged?" I asked with a laugh.

He smiled. "Yeah. When I kissed you, I never felt that much passion from someone else."

"Well, you are a really good kisser. And I do like you."

Tony's eyes shined brighter. He leaned closer to me, clearly pleased with that response. "I'm glad to hear that."

"I'm assuming you have sex on a regular basis?"

"Uh, not necessarily."

"Have you been in a serious relationship recently?"

"No. It's been a long time."

"So you just date people?"

"On and off," he said.

I wanted to ask him if it was because he was rich but I decided not to. He clearly didn't like discussing that. I could understand why. When it came to money, people were weird. And I'm sure he had girls date him just to get a chance at his money. It was difficult to tell if people really liked him for who he was. I didn't care about his money. I was falling for him because he was a great guy, the first great guy I met in years.

The waiter brought our food and we ate quietly. Tony had perfect table manners. That didn't surprise me at all. He ate his pizza with a knife and a fork rather than holding it by the slice. When we were done, the waiter brought the tab.

"Let me get it this time," I said. "You paid for all that junk food the other night."

He stared at me like I just burped out a frog. "What?"

"Let's trade off."

"That's the first time I've been out with a girl who's ever offered to pay."

"Oh," I said. "Well, I think that's fair. I guess I'm a feminist."

He stared at me for a long time before he threw the cash in. "My dates don't pay for their meals."

"Can I get the tip?"

"No," he snapped.

I backed down.

"I'm sorry," he said. "I didn't mean to go overboard."

I said nothing.

"Are you ready to go?"

"Yes."

We left the restaurant then walked back to my apartment. When we reached the door, I didn't want him to leave. I already really liked him. I knew I had to tell Janet the truth soon. I was falling for her brother and I couldn't do that behind her back. She was my best friend.

He stared at me then placed his hand on my lower back. "I don't mean to be forward but could we be exclusive?"

"Oh," I said. "I assumed that we were."

"Good," he said. "I don't want you dating anyone else."

"The feeling is mutual."

He leaned in and kissed me gently, making an involuntary gasp escape my lips. I wrapped my arms around his neck and kissed him aggressively, loving the feel of his lips on my own. Being close to him made me feel excited and nervous at the same time. I didn't want him to leave. I didn't want this night to end.

"Come inside," I whispered.

He rubbed his nose against mine. "Okay."

I opened the door then placed my purse and keys on the table.

Tony came behind me and grabbed me by the neck. "Do you masturbate?"

My cheeks blushed at his question.

He stared at me, waiting for me to respond.

I nodded.

"Then why are you so hot?"

"Because you're hot," I said with a light laugh. "And that isn't the same as a real man. I haven't had it in so long. I didn't realize how much I missed it until now. You're the first guy that I met who I actually like. That's rare for me. Maybe I'm just picky. But you make me feel…hot."

He pulled me to his chest. "I would love to give you an orgasm."

My spine shivered at his words. "I don't do this very often."

"What?"

"Sleep with a guy that I've only dated for a week."

"I figured."

"Do you think I'm a slut?"

"Not at all," he said as he looked into my face. "You're human with biological instincts. You're really attracted to me. That's natural. And I'm really attracted to you. And it wouldn't be a one night stand. I want this to go somewhere."

"I do too."

He kissed me gently, making my lips burn. Now that I knew where this would lead, I let my primal desire surface. I gripped his shoulders and kissed him passionately, letting myself lose control. I couldn't wait months after being in a relationship to have sex, and I couldn't have sex with a guy I didn't really like. I want Tony. I wanted him now.

He guided me toward my bedroom while he kissed me. When we entered my room, he laid me on the bed then moved on top of me. Feeling the soft sheets under my skin made me moan. The area between my legs was on fire.

Tony kissed my neck then the skin on top of my breasts. His hand moved up my dress until he felt my underwear. He played with it before he unzipped my dress and pulled it off. I didn't feel self-conscious in my bra and underwear. He looked at me with heat in his eyes. The gaze made me feel attractive. He kissed my inner thighs then pulled down my thong. When his lips kissed me down there, I moaned loudly. I hadn't been touched there in so long. His tongue moved across my folds and moved inside me. It felt unbelievable. Then he unclasped my bra and looked at my breasts. He kissed each one, gliding his tongue across the nipples.

I was enjoying this but I wanted to see him. He hadn't shed any clothing. I grabbed his shirt and pulled it off. His naked chest was hard as stone. The pectoral muscles were wide and powerful, and his stomach had a deep valley and grooves. My hands glided over it, treasuring the sight.

His unbuttoned his jeans then pulled them off. When he was just in his boxers, I grabbed the rim and pulled them down. His cock sprang out, big and long.

"Oh…wow."

He moved on top of me and kissed me again. It was gentle and soft, the caresses leaving me shaking. I never tasted something I loved so much. I gripped the back of his neck and slipped my tongue inside. It touched his, sending shivers through my body. He was such a good kisser.

Tony pulled away. "Do you have a condom?"

"Oh." I kissed his neck because I couldn't stop. My hands were gliding over his chest. "In my nightstand."

He opened it and picked up a packet. After he ripped it open, I grabbed it and rolled it onto his impressive length. I left plenty of room for him at the tip then rolled the latex down to the base. Just doing this made me feel the orgasm in the recesses of my body.

Tony pulled my hips toward him then leaned over me. "You're beautiful," he whispered.

I gripped his back, preparing for the impact. I grabbed his face and kissed him, my mouth being pleasured by his. When I felt the beginning stretch, I moaned loudly. He moved inside slowly until he was completely sheathed. "Oh my god…"

Tony cupped my face and stared into my eyes while he moved slowly.

I was so overwhelmed with the pleasure that I couldn't do anything. I just dug my nails into his skin, feeling him move inside me. "Tony…yeah."

He moved a little faster but kept it gentle. His eyes were on mine the while time, watching my expression from above. Tony kissed me every few seconds, staying connected to me while he rocked together. Within seconds, I was there. Just from the buildup, I knew this orgasm was going to be the best one I had in a long time. It was hot and fiery, igniting my body in a blaze.

"Oh…yeah….oh." My head rolled back as it hit me. I gripped him tighter.

Tony moved faster, making me feel as good as possible.

When I was done, I was out of breath. There was sweat on my chest and it dripped to my stomach.

Tony thrust until he met his bliss. He gripped my face and pressed his forehead against mind as he came, moaning the entire time. "Mmmm…." He stopped then kissed me gently.

I wrapped my arms around his neck then ran my fingers through his hair.

When he pulled out, he rolled the condom off then tossed it in the garbage.

I sighed deeply. "Thank you. Thank you."

He smiled then lied beside me. "I'm glad I could help."

I crawled on his chest then looked down at him. "That felt so amazing. That was the best sex I've ever had."

"Thank you. I like what I'm hearing."

I kissed him then snuggled next to him. "You're so good."

"I think it's just because you haven't had it in so long."

'No, Tony. You are amazing."

He turned on his side and pulled me to his chest. "I like these compliments."

"I feel so much better now. I was going crazy for a while there."

"My services are always available to you."

"I think I'll take advantage of that."

"Good. I was hoping you would."

I wrapped my arm around his waist then stared at him. I realized he probably wanted to leave. Guys never liked to cuddle. "You can go if you want. I understand that you have other things you need to do."

"I don't," he said. "And I would rather stay here with you anyway."

My eyes softened. "I guess I should tell Janet about us."

"Don't," he said.

"Why not?" I asked.

"It's none of her business. That's why."

I stared at him. "Are you embarrassed of me or something?"

"Not at all," he said. "I just don't want my sister to be weird about us. She's always been protective of me. She didn't introduce us for a reason. I don't want to know what that reason is. I really like you and you make me happy. Let's just be happy."

"But I'm lying to my best friend."

"We'll tell her eventually. I don't like being deceitful. Actually, I hate it. And I don't care what people think. But I do care what my sister thinks. You're just too good to be true. I don't want to lose you."

"I don't want to lose you either."

"I've been dating for years and I haven't found anyone. Some of the girls were cool, but none of them got me excited. Not the way you do. If this doesn't work out, I want to treasure what we have in the moment."

I stared at his face and looked at his beautiful eyes. "I really like you too."

He came close to me, his breaths falling on my face. "Is it cool if I sleep here?"

"You want to sleep with me?"

"Of course I do."

I smiled. "I would love that."

"Good. Because I wasn't going to leave if you said no. After that performance, I'm exhausted."

"You didn't even last that long," I teased.

"Hey," he said. "Do you know how hard it is not to come when the girl you're making love to is enjoying it so much? It's really difficult."

"So you're blaming it on me?" I said with a laugh.

"Yep."

"And we were making love?"

"We certainly weren't fucking. I don't fuck girls I like."

I wasn't expecting that. "You're really sweet, Tony."

"I'm not, actually."

"I find that hard to believe."

"I'm sweet when I care about someone. And even then, I'm not that nice. Just ask my sister."

I laughed. "You have a point."

He grabbed his phone and set the alarm. "Do you make breakfast in the morning?"

"I can," I said.

"I just need coffee."

"I can do that."

He kissed me on the cheek. "Goodnight, Cassie."

"Goodnight." I listened to the sound of his breathing before I fell asleep.

6

"I can tell you got laid," Orlando said.

I blushed then shut the door. "Keep your voice down." Tony and I had been dating for a month. The sex was great and I couldn't get enough of it. But my joy and satisfaction was evident to everyone around me. Orlando finally picked up on it.

"How was it?"

"Amazing," I said. "It felt so good."

"So he rocked your world?"

"Definitely," I said.

"I have to see what this guy looks like," he said.

"He said he wanted to be exclusive so I guess we could do on a double date."

"What does exclusive mean?" he asked.

"We don't see other people."

He rolled his eyes. "I know that. Does that mean you're in a relationship?"

"I don't think so. We're just dating but not dating other people. I really like him, Orlando. *A lot*."

"He sounds like the real deal."

"He doesn't want to tell his sister though."

"Why?" he asked.

"He says she might be weird about it and break us up."

"I wonder why."

I shrugged. "He said she's protective of him."

Orlando sat down and spun around in the chair. "Do you think Janet won't want you to date him because you aren't good enough for him?"

That made me sad. "I hope not."

"Or maybe it's the other way around," Orlando said. "Maybe he's a jerk."

"I doubt it," I said. "He's a huge sweetheart."

Orlando stared at my face. "You're totally falling for him."

"I already did," I said.

He laughed. "At least you admit it."

Winnie and Gloria walked out of the changing rooms with the new gowns I designed. I stared at them with approval.

"She'll love them," Orlando said. "I would wear them if I knew I wouldn't be shot."

I laughed. "Thanks."

Gloria spun around. "I hope Pia doesn't like it so I can take it home."

"If she doesn't like it, I'm going to scream," I said.

Orlando peeked down the hallway. "She's coming," he whispered.

Pia walked inside, looking pissed as usual. Her assistant's face was stoic and blank. They both looked like statues, not animated or interested in any way.

Pia walked around the dresses and made the models stand in different poses. I waited patiently while she searched for things I couldn't see. It was hard to tell if she liked what she saw. She had the best poker face in the world. "No."

"No?"

She glared at me.

"What's wrong with them?"

"You call this fashion?" she snapped.

I kept my anger back. I wanted to keep my job so I remained calm. "Please let me know what you're looking for. I will deliver."

"You're the fashion designer," she said while she stared me down. "It's your responsibility to create pieces of art, not me. Don't give me that attitude again. Get it right next time or I'll find you a replacement." She walked out with her assistant trailing behind her.

I wanted to scream.

Orlando immediately came to my side. "We'll figure it out."

"This is bullshit," I snapped.

Gloria and Winnie both look frightened. They never heard me get upset before.

"I should just quit," I said. "I hate working her anyway."

"Don't go crazy," Orlando said. "Just sleep on it and we'll go from there."

I marched into my office and slammed the door. I took deep breaths and controlled my anger. Without knowing what to do to survive the rest of the day, I called Tony. We hadn't been dating long, but he was already the closest person to me. The sex was amazing, the conversation was unforced, and he was just an awesome guy. I loved spending time with him. He was starting to mean more than he did ever before. He was my greatest lover and my best friend.

"Hey," he said. "Is everything alright?"

"I'm just having a stressful day at work."

"Do you want to talk about it?"

"No."

"Okay," he said. "The Rangers are playing next week. You're coming, right?"

"I'll be there."

"I got you something today."

"What is it?"

"It's a surprise."

"Come on. Spill it."

"I got you a Rangers jersey. Now we match."

"That's so cute," I said.

"Am I going to get some hot sex out of it?"

"You were going to get hot sex either way."

"You're so awesome."

He already made me feel better. "How's your day?"

"It's okay. A little boring."

"What time do you get off work?"

"Well, I work from home so whenever."

I still didn't understand what he did for a living. It seemed like nothing.

"Can I see you tonight?" he asked.

"I'm going out with the girls."

"That's right," he said. "Scott mentioned it."

"We should tell Janet soon."

He sighed. "I know."

"I'll talk to her tonight."

"No, have fun. We'll do it together sometime."

"Okay," I said. "Well, I should go. Thank you for making me feel better."

"Always."

"Bye."

"Bye."

After I went home and changed, I went to the bar to meet Layla and Janet. When I sat down with them at the table, I immediately felt awkward. It was hard keeping such a big secret from my two best friends. And I felt like I was betraying Janet.

"You don't look happy," Layla said.

"I had a bad day at work," I said.

"What happened?" Janet asked.

"My boss doesn't like anything I make and basically threatened to fire me if I don't get it right next time."

"Then do as she asks," Janet said.

"It's not that simple," I said. "She gives me absolutely no feedback. It's basically a process of trial and error."

"I'm sorry," Janet said. "Your drinks are on me."

I smiled. "That's nice of you, especially since I'm about to be broke."

Layla looked at me. "Kyle can get you a job at Satin Magazine if you really need it."

"Thank you," I said. "But I'll figure it out."

"Can we join you?" Scott said.

We turned to see him standing there, a beer in his hand.

"What are you doing here?" Janet asked.

"Tony and I just came here to watch the game."

Janet rolled her eyes. "Don't you have any other friends?"

He came to her and kissed her gently. That shut her up.

My heart raced when I realized Tony was there.

"Hello," he said as he came to the table. He looked at me first, his eyes moving over my body then back to my face. He turned to his sister. "Hey, sis."

She glared at him. "I'm so pissed at you."

He looked alarmed. "Why?"

"You convinced Scott to gamble ten thousand dollars!"

Tony laughed. "What's the big deal? He won."

"That doesn't matter," she snapped. "I don't want Scott to ruin his life savings."

"Well, it's his money," Tony said. "He can do whatever he wants."

She glared at him again.

"Are you going to introduce me to your friends?" he asked.

She sighed. "This is my brother, Tony."

I looked at him. "Hi."

He nodded.

Layla shook his hand. "It's nice to meet you."

"You too," Tony said. He took a seat at the table directly across from me. It was hard for me not to stare at him. I wanted to kiss him or embrace him in some way.

Janet looked at her brother. "How's it going with Jasmine?"

He looked uncomfortable. "We stopped dating a while ago."

"You just went out with her a few weeks ago."

My heart clenched painfully.

"It was a month ago," he corrected. "I haven't seen her since."

"What was wrong with her?" she asked. "You were dating for a while."

"She wasn't the right person." He looked at me then turned away.

Now I wondered if he had been dating her while he was dating me. I really hoped not. I'd grown very attached to Tony. I loved spending time with him, going to the games with him, out to dinner, and sleeping with him.

Scott's glance kept moving back and forth between us. I wondered if Tony told him the truth.

"Why haven't you introduced me to your friends before this?" Tony asked, changing the subject.

She looked away. "No reason. It just didn't happen."

Tony didn't look convinced.

Scott wrapped his arm around Janet's shoulder. "Do you want anything at the bar?"

"I'm okay, babe."

I felt sick to my stomach so I left the table and went to the bar. I needed a moment. If I went to the bathroom, everyone would know something was bothering me. Now it looked like I just wanted another drink.

When I sat down, I ordered a scotch.

Tony appeared at my side a moment later. "I wasn't dating her at the same time," he said without preamble.

"It sounds like it," I said without looking at him.

He stood over me, very close to my arm. "I was dating her the first time we went out. After the game, I knew how much I liked you. When I went home, I broke it off with her. We were never exclusive, but I felt guilty dating her while I was dating you. And that's why I didn't kiss you. I felt like that would be disrespectful to both of you."

I finally looked at him. "Really?"

"That's the truth."

"Okay."

"You believe me?"

I nodded.

"We're okay?"

"Yeah."

He breathed a sigh of relief. "I was scared for a second."

"You haven't been seeing anyone else, right?"

His eyes narrowed. "Of course not. I said we were exclusive. And I'm with you all the time. When would I have time to date someone else?"

"I'm sorry I said that."

"It's okay," he said. "I know you've had a rough day."

I drank my glass then ordered another. "Does Scott know about us?"

He nodded. "He said he wouldn't tell her."

"I don't think I can keep this up any longer. I just want to be honest about it."

"Give it some more time."

"What are you waiting for?"

"Let's just wait a little bit."

I sighed. "Well, you should go back to the table so it doesn't look suspicious."

"It's hard for me to leave you when you seem upset."

"I'm fine, Tony."

"Okay." He walked away and returned to the table. I downed another scotch then swallowed the bitter aftertaste.

"Cassie?"

I turned in my seat. "Danny?" My heart stopped beating altogether. I hadn't seen him in almost two years. I never ran into him on the subway or at a restaurant. I thought I would never run into him. And that's what I wanted. To never see him again.

He sat in the chair next to me. "How are you?"

"I'm good," I lied.

Danny stared at me with the gray eyes I used to love. "I'm glad you're well."

"Yeah…" Now I just wanted him to walk away. There was nothing to say.

"Are you seeing anyone?"

I didn't know what answer I should give. I was seeing someone but he was a secret. And I didn't know if he would ever not be a secret. He was standing in this very bar but I couldn't acknowledge him as such. "No."

He eyes shined a little brighter. "Are you still a fashion designer?"

For now. "Yes."

"That good to hear."

"How are you and Emily?"

He averted his gaze when I said her name.

"She had to come up at some point, right?"

"She and I broke up a few months ago."

"Oh," I said. "I'm sorry." Actually, I wasn't sorry. But I felt like a bitch saying that.

"She left me for someone else."

"Karma's a bitch, isn't it?" It flew out of my mouth before I could stop it.

"I deserved that," he said quietly.

"So, who are you dating now?"

"No one," he said. "I've been single for a while."

I stared at my empty glass.

"Can I get you another?"

"No, I've had enough."

"Are you alone?" he asked.

"No, I'm here with my friends. I just wanted to take a break from their chit-chat."

"You know, I would love to take you to coffee," he said. "I feel like we never really had a chance to talk after—you know."

"My number hasn't changed," I said. "You could have called me whenever you wanted."

His eyes sagged. "I know."

"So, I don't think there's anything for us to talk about."

"I would still love to see you."

"I've been nice this long, but my politeness is wearing thin, Danny. I'll never give you a second chance. And if your request is genuine and you want to spend time with me as a friend, I don't want that either. You obviously have no respect for me after what you did."

He nodded. "That's fair."

"So just go, please."

Danny didn't move.

Tony came to my side and wrapped his arm around me. The heat from his hand almost burned my skin. He came close to me, touching me possessively. I felt the intimidation leak out of him. His eyes burned with hatred. "Baby, is this guy bothering you?"

Danny moved away slightly.

"No," I said.

Danny looked relieved.

"It didn't look like it," he said. He kept glaring at Danny. "Get the fuck away from her."

A few people at the bar turned toward us.

Danny looked at him. "She said she doesn't have a boyfriend, so you're obviously the one bothering her."

Tony looked at me. "You said that?"

"Well...I didn't know what to say. Janet is here..."

Tony didn't look pleased. "I'll repeat myself one time. Get the hell away from her or I'll beat the shit out of you."

Danny stood up then brushed Tony's shoulder as he passed. He turned around and looked at me. "I'll call you."

Tony threw a punch quicker than I could see.

Danny was on the ground, gripping his nose as the blood came out.

"What did you say?" Tony said as he stood over him.

Danny got to his feet. "Fuck you, asshole."

"If you contact her, I'll kill you."

Danny left the bar. It was quiet for a moment before people starting talking again. Tony came back to me, the look of anger still etched on his face.

"What the fuck was that about? You were going to date him?"

"No!"

"Then why would you say you're single?"

"I already said why."

Janet came over to us. "What was that about?"

Tony dropped his hand from my side. "Nothing."

"But you punched—"

"Shut up, Janet."

She flinched at the hostility in his voice.

Tony marched out of the bar without looking back.

7

I understood why Tony was mad, but I didn't have a chance to explain myself, especially with Janet standing there. A part of me was angry at him because the incident wouldn't have happened if we weren't keeping our relationship a secret.

I called him a few times but he didn't answer. I would have gone to his apartment but I didn't know where he lived. My bad day just went from really bad to worse. I called him again. When the voicemail picked up, I left a message.

"Tony, Tyler is standing outside my door and he won't go away. He keeps knocking and he won't stop. I'm scared and I don't know what to do." I hung up.

I felt guilty for lying but I knew it would work.

In less than ten minutes, he was banging on the door. "Cassie! Are you there?" He banged his fist again.

I answered it.

He stormed inside. "Are you okay?"

"I'm fine."

"Where the fuck is he?"

I shut the door and stood in front of it. "Tyler isn't here and he never was here."

His eyes widened. "What?"

"I made it up."

He glared at me. "You tricked me?"

"I want to explain what happened."

Tony shook his head. "I know exactly what happened. You were picking up guys in bars while we were dating. Why would you do that? We were happy together. Did you think I wouldn't notice?"

"Tony, shut the hell up and listen to me."

"It looks like I don't have a choice."

"Danny is my ex-boyfriend."

His eyes narrowed.

"And when he asked if I had a boyfriend, I didn't want to say I did if I couldn't prove it. It would be like I was lying, and I didn't want him to think I was saying that because I was miserable or something. So, I just said no. Of course I wasn't going to go out with him. I was asking him to leave."

Tony paced in front of me. "I—I didn't know that."

"I wish I could just be honest and tell people we are dating. That's what I want, Tony. You're the one stopping us from doing that. Not me. So if anyone should be upset, it's me."

He sighed. "You're right."

"I know I am."

"We'll talk to her soon."

"What the hell does that mean?"

"Very soon," he said.

I moved away from the door so he could leave. "Goodnight, Tony."

"I'm not leaving." He locked the door and came back to me.

"I don't want you here."

He circled his arms around me and held me to his chest. "I'm sorry."

I stared at his chest.

His lips brushed my ear. "Baby, come on."

"Baby?"

"Yeah."

"That sounds like a name couples use."

"We are a couple."

"No we aren't," I said.

"I want to be one."

I stared at him. "I'm not going to be your girlfriend. Nothing changes."

His eyes sagged. "Cassie, I really like you. I want to be something more with you."

"Only if you tell your sister the truth."

He sighed. "That's fair."

"I know it is."

Tony held me to his chest then ran his fingers through my hair. "This has been a really bad day."

"It has."

"I wish I brought your jersey over to cheer you up."

"That would have been nice."

He pulled away and kissed my forehead. "Can I sleep with you tonight? I miss you."

I didn't know what was going on anymore. I loved being with Tony. He was perfect in every way. I wanted to be in a real relationship. It seemed like he did too. "No."

His eyes lost their light. "I said I was sorry and I meant it."

"I don't know anything about you."

"What are you talking about? You know me better than anyone else."

"I've never seen your apartment. I don't know what you do for a living. You won't tell me that you're loaded and you keep trying to hide it from me. You won't tell your sister about me. This isn't real, Tony. We're just fucking around."

"No, we aren't," he said firmly. "I care about you, Cassie. This isn't a fling."

"Well, it seems like it is."

"I only had sex with you because you wanted me to. I would have waited as long as you wanted."

"That isn't what I meant either."

"Cassie, what do you want?"

"I want the truth. I want you to tell your sister about us and I want to know what you're hiding. If that's not something you can do, I want to end this—relationship— and act like it never happened."

He sighed. "Okay."

"What does that mean?"

"I agree to your terms." He grabbed my face to kiss me but I pulled away. "Fine. I guess it will have to wait."

"Goodnight, Tony."

"Do you want to do it together?"

I nodded.

"Tomorrow, then."

"Okay."

8

Tony came over the next evening.

When I opened the door, I didn't have a smile on my face like I usually did.

He embraced me but I pulled away. "Why are you acting like this?" he asked.

I grabbed my purse and kept my gaze averted.

"Look at me," she snapped.

I met his gaze.

"We're telling her the truth. I want you to kiss me and I want you to hug me when I walk through that door."

"We haven't told her yet."

"I said I would."

"You might change your mind."

He grabbed my arm and came closer to me. "You gave me an ultimatum. If I don't tell my sister, I lose you. That's something I can't afford to lose. I gamble all the time, but I never gamble more than I can afford. I can't lose you. I can't."

I walked to the door and turned around.

Tony remained glued to the spot, breathing through his frustration. He came back to me a moment later. We left the building and went to Scott's apartment on the other side of town. Tony tried to hold my hand in the cab but I pulled it away.

When we reached their door, I looked at him. "Are you sure you want to do this?"

"I don't want you to lose you, Cassie."

"Why would you?"

He sighed. "I'm afraid of what my sister is going to say. It's not about taking our relationship public. It's about how it might affect us."

"What do you mean?"

"I don't know…"

"Yes, you do."

"I'm not a noble person. I made my money doing illegal things. She might tell you to ditch me because I'm not good enough for you."

"Tony, do you kill people?"

"No," he said quickly.

"Then I don't care what illegal things you did."

He sighed. "My sister doesn't feel the same way."

"Well, I don't care."

"That gives me some relief."

"Let's get this over with."

He knocked on the door.

Scott answered it. "Hey," he said when he saw Tony. When he looked at me said, "Oh."

Tony nodded. "Janet here?"

"Yeah, come in."

We walked inside and stood a few feet apart.

Janet came into the living room. "What are you guys doing here?"

Tony cleared his throat. "We just came by to visit."

She eyed him suspiciously. "You already see Scott all the time. Do you really need to be with him 24/7?"

Tony ignored the comment. "Let's sit down."

"Okay…"

We went into the living room and took our places. When Tony sat next to me, he kept his hands to himself. I didn't show any affection either.

Janet eyed us. "Why are both of you here?"

I said nothing, letting Tony do all the talking.

Tony looked at his sister. "I want to talk to you about something."

"What?" she asked. "What's wrong?"

"There's nothing wrong," he said. "In fact, I have good news. Basically, Janet and I have been dating for a month. She and I really hit it off and we enjoy being together. The longer this has gone on, the more serious it has become. We just wanted to come clean about it."

Janet stared at him for a long time but said nothing. Then she looked at me. "Why didn't you tell me?"

"I asked her not to," Tony said.

"Why?" she asked.

"Because I know how protective you are. And I also know that you intentionally didn't introduce me to your friends. I'm not sure why but I'm sure there's a reason."

Janet looked at Scott. "Did you know about this?"

"No," Tony answered. "I didn't tell him."

Scott looked relieved.

"And nothing you say will change our relationship," Tony said. "All Cassie and I are asking for is your acceptance. She and I are ready to be serious and public. We don't want to hide it anymore."

Janet crossed her legs then uncrossed them, clearly flustered. "A month?"

Tony nodded.

"You've been seeing each over for a whole month and you didn't say anything?"

"Yes," Tony answered.

I still hadn't spoken but I didn't have anything to say. It seemed like Tony could handle his sister.

"I'm upset that you didn't tell me," she said.

"I know," Tony said. "And I understand why."

She glared at him. "Have you slept together?"

Scott turned to her. "Baby, that's none of our business."

"Yes, we have," Tony answered.

I felt my cheeks blush.

Janet turned her eyes on me. "I can't believe you would date and fuck my brother without talking to me first." The anger in her eyes was palpable. "That crosses so many lines, Cassie. You're my best friend. I trusted you. This is just wrong."

"Like I said, she wanted to say something but I told her not to," Tony said. "This is entirely my fault."

Janet shook her head. "It doesn't excuse her behavior. She lied to me for a whole month. That's unacceptable."

"Janet, I'm sorry," I said quietly. "I wanted to tell you—"

"But you didn't," she snapped. "You fucked my brother repeatedly and didn't say a single thing to me. You understand how much Tony means to me. Outside of the of you and Layla, he's my best friend."

"I know," I said. "And I wouldn't hurt him. I really care about him."

Janet shook her head. "This would be totally different if you asked me beforehand."

"I know," I whispered.

Tony looked mad. "Janet, shut the hell up. Cassie said she was sorry. Now get over it. She and I are together and we're happy. You'll have to deal with that."

Janet glared at her brother. "I want to talk to you outside."

"No," he snapped. He grabbed my hand. "I'm not going anywhere without her. Whatever you want to say to me, you can say it in front of my girlfriend."

I sighed. Tony had predicted this situation perfectly. I had no idea Janet would be so upset. I didn't see what the fuss was about. I was her best friend. Wasn't I the best person for her brother? Wouldn't that be ideal?"

"Fine," Janet said. "I don't want you to date Cassie."

That made my heart shatter. I couldn't believe she said that.

"Why?" Tony asked.

"You know why."

"It changes nothing," he said.

"Yes, it does," she said. "Cassie isn't right for you. I'm doing this to protect you."

I felt the tears bubble under my eyes. "Why am I not good enough for him?"

Tony looked at me and squeezed my hand. "You are, baby."

Janet didn't look at me. "End this relationship. If you don't, I won't be friends with Cassie anymore, Scott won't be friends with you, and you and I can stop talking."

"Are you fucking kidding me?" Tony said, standing up.

Janet met his look with a stoic expression. "I'm being dead serious."

"Fuck you! You're my best friend. How can you be so selfish and act like this?"

Janet shook her head. "You know I love you. You know I have to protect you. And if that makes me lose the people I care about, then so be it. But I would do anything and everything for you. Don't date Cassie."

Tony stared at her incredulously. "I can't believe you. I finally found someone I like and I'm supposed to believe she's a greedy gold digger? That doesn't make any sense. You wouldn't be friends with her if that's how she was."

Janet ignored his comment. "If you break up, everything will go back to the way it was. I'll still be best friends with Cassie, and our relationship won't change. I suggest you make the right decision."

Tony shook his head. "No."

"Fine," Janet said. "You can see yourself out."

Tony's hands started to shake. "Come on, Cassie."

I stared at Janet without moving. "I would never hurt your brother, Janet."

She didn't look at me. "It's nothing personal, Cassie."

"Obviously, it is," I said.

"Please leave my brother alone."

"I really care about him. I don't care about his money. I'm not using him."

"Cassie, you hate working and you've always wanted to be a housewife. I know what you're doing."

I felt the blow slice right through my heart. "That isn't what's going on here."

Janet looked away.

"Babe, let's go," Tony said as he grabbed my hand. He pulled me from the apartment then slammed the door shut. "I'm so sorry."

I felt the tears fall. "I can't believe she thinks I would ever do that."

"Don't let it bother you," he said as he held me.

"How can I not?"

He kissed my tears away. "She's being a bitch. Forget her."

"She's my best friend."

"Let's go to my apartment. It's closer." He took me by the hand and we left for his building. I wasn't watching where we were going. I kept replaying the conversation in my mind. I finally found a guy I really liked. And he was my best friend's brother. But it turned out for the worst. I couldn't have him.

When we walked inside his apartment, I looked around. It was on the top floor of a nice building. It was huge, almost the size of my whole floor. There were windows that reached from the ceiling to the floor. Every piece of furniture looked more expensive than a car. To say it was nice was an understatement.

Tony grabbed me and kissed me. "I don't care what my sister thinks, Cassie."

"She's your sister. Yes, you do."

He shook his head. "I'm not negotiating with her."

"And I'm not coming between you."

He tightened his grip on my waist. "I'm not letting you go. You can run but I'll catch you. We aren't ending this relationship."

"But I can't do that to you."

"You didn't do anything. She's causing all this strife."

More tears fell down my face.

Tony looked at me. "Let's get in the shower."

I was too upset to argue. I was a walking zombie.

When Tony stripped off his clothes and got inside, I noticed the beauty of his physique. It normally made my veins singe with arousal, but right now I was too upset to feel anything. We both got inside and stood under the water. He held me to his chest while I cried. I hated crying and I hardly ever did it, but I was falling apart. I had to choose between my best friend and my boyfriend.

Tony placed his face against mine and kissed my tears away. He stared at me with a sad expression. "I'm so sorry."

"I'm so sorry too."

"You did nothing wrong, Cassie."

"I'm not with you because of your money," I blurted.

"I know. I never thought that."

"I just want to make sure you realize that."

He nodded.

After I calmed down, he turned off the shower and dried me off. His touch was gentle as he patted me down. Then he picked me up and carried me into his bedroom. It had a large king size bed in the center with a large walk in closest and a separate bathroom. When I lay on the sheets, I sighed. It was so soft.

He came beside me and pulled the covers over us. It wasn't that late, but neither one of us were in the mood to do anything. We were both too depressed.

"I need to uphold the second half of my bargain."

I looked at him, waiting for him to elaborate.

"A few years ago, I had a girlfriend. She seemed really cool and I liked her. But I eventually realized she only wanted me for my money. That's what she wanted all along. I was pretty hurt by it and my sister had to see me go through that. In that respect, I understand why she's so protective of me. She doesn't want me to go through that again. I'm not defending her. I'm just explaining."

"I know," I whispered.

"I started gambling when I was in college. It started off small, but after I won a few times, I became addicted. I've always been obsessed with sports so I was pretty knowledgeable about everything. My small wins became bigger and bigger. Then I started playing with the big boys.

My addiction only grew. I ended up making enough money
that I bought the Rangers."

"You *bought* the Rangers?"

He nodded.

"Well, that explains a lot."

"I'm always quiet about my profession because
people want in on it, or they want money from me. So
dating is really hard. I always have to act broke or like an
average Joe."

"Is that why you took me to the Ranger game?"

He smiled. "I've always wanted a girl that loves
sports, and someone who doesn't care about fancy dinners
and bullshit like that. When we went to the game you had
so much fun. I could tell you didn't care that I wasn't
taking you to the Ritz. I was immediately smitten with you.
I knew you were the one for me. And when we went to
dinner and you offered to pay, I was shocked. Girls never

140

do that. I wouldn't want you to pay, but it's nice to be in a relationship where I know I'm not being used."

I nodded. "I can understand that. And when I told Janet that I wanted to be a housewife, I meant when I have kids. Not forever."

"You don't have to explain yourself," he said gently.

"I just don't want you to think that's why I'm around."

"You've already proven it to me," he said. "I see the way you look at me. There's nothing but love there."

"What should we do?" I asked with a sigh.

"We're staying together."

"But—"

"No buts. If my sister wants to behave this way, fine. I don't care. I'm not giving you up. You did nothing wrong."

I still wasn't convinced. "But she's my best friend."

"I know," he said gently. "But she isn't tearing us apart. She'll realize she's wrong eventually."

"And if she doesn't?"

He shrugged. "It's her loss."

I stared at his chest and thought to myself. This was a bad situation. I wished it never happened. Tony made me so happy and I didn't want to give him up. And he was right about Janet. Her assumptions were completely wrong. I was seriously wounded by the horrible accusations. She couldn't be more wrong.

Tony moved on top of me then pinned my legs back. "I'm not going anywhere."

"I really don't want to lose you."

"You won't," he said as he pressed his face close to mine. He slid inside me and made me moan.

"Tony…"

"I'm not giving this up for anything," he whispered in my ear. He moved inside me, his hands holding my legs

142

back. Tony stared into my eyes while he made love to me. It felt amazing every time we were together, more amazing than I ever could have dreamed. I grabbed the back of his neck and felt more tears fall. Tony was everything to me, the person I always wanted. I couldn't let him go. If I did, it would break my heart.

"Look at me," he whispered.

I opened my eyes and looked into his.

He kissed the moisture around my eyes while he thrust.

I felt myself tighten around him as my body gave into him. The pleasure spread through my body and ignited me, making me burn like hot ash. "Tony…."

"Baby…"

"Yeah…god yeah."

He stiffed as he met his bliss at the same time. He moved into me a few more times before we were both finished. His hands grabbed my neck and he kissed me gently, trailing kisses everywhere. When he pulled out, he grabbed me and pulled me to his chest, holding me close. I never felt more depressed and happy at the same time. But as long as I had Tony, I would be okay. Janet is the one who ruined everything. When my depression faded away, all I felt was rage.

9

I was pretty depressed for the next few days. I kept checking my phone to see if Janet called but she never did. It was the hardest breakup I'd ever been through. I never lost a girlfriend, especially one I was so close to. I knew I shouldn't be sad because Janet was out of line, but I couldn't help it. I missed her.

When I told Orlando everything, he was pissed.

"Fuck that cunt," he said.

"Keep your voice down," I whispered.

"I can't believe her. At least Tony had your back."

"Yeah," I said. "He refused to break up."

"He really likes you, Cassie."

"And I really like him.'"

"No, you love him," Orlando said.

"No, I don't."

He rolled his eyes. "Whatever."

"But I'm starting to."

Pia hadn't given me another assignment for the magazine so I had a short break to get everything together for the next piece. I did extensive research on the fashion hit in Milan and Paris. She expected me to pick upcoming fashion trends before they happened, which was just ridiculous. I went to school so I could recognize trends and improve them. I wasn't a fortune teller. I seriously hated my boss. The only good thing about this place was Orlando. He was a godsend to me.

When I went to Tony's that night, he had his friends over for the game.

"Hey, baby," he said when he opened the door. He kissed me and made my lips burn. "I'm glad you're here."

I held up a six pack. "And I bring gifts."

"Ooh. Now you're even better." He grabbed it and put it on the table.

When I took off my jacket, he saw the Ranger jersey he got me. We were watching baseball but I wanted to wear it anyway.

"You look so fucking cute in that."

I smiled. "You like it?"

"I want to make love tonight while you wear this."

"I can do that."

He pulled me close to him and gave me another kiss. The guys in the living room cheered when the Yankees scored. "Let me introduce you to the guys." We walked into the living room and he introduced me to everyone. They were all nice and friendly. I felt a little out of place being the only girl there, but Tony made sure I wasn't lonely.

When he sat on the couch, he pulled me into his lap and held me close. There was plenty of room to sit, but he didn't want me anywhere else. Scott came over and sat next to us.

I looked at him. "I thought you weren't supposed to talk to us?"

Scott drank from his beer. "She can't tell me what to do. I don't care if she's mad."

"You won't be getting any tonight," Tony said.

"I don't care," Scott said. "I'm pretty fucking pissed at her."

I breathed a sigh of relief. "So you don't think I'm with Tony for his money?"

"Not at all," he said. "And I'm shocked that your best friend doesn't see it either."

Talking about Janet was making me depressed.

Scott continued talking. "Life is too short and precious to cut people out of your life forever. I know Janet means well, but this is a stupid way to go about it. My parents died years ago so I know what it's like to lose someone you can't get back. It just gets under my skin…"

"I hope you can change her mind," I said.

"Me too."

Tony moved his hand through my hair while he watched the TV. When a commercial was on, his eyes were only for me. He pulled me close to him and kissed me like he hadn't felt my lips in years. His hand moved under my jersey and felt the skin of my stomach. I felt like his obsession. He couldn't get enough of me.

When the game was over, the guys stayed over and ate pizza and hot wings. I could tell Tony was close with his friends because he was carefree and natural around them. Before he told me the truth, he was always slightly rigid and closed off. Now he was different, happy. He didn't have to hide.

After everyone left, I helped him clean everything up. There were beer bottles, plates, and pizza boxes everywhere. It was a total mess. When everything was put away, we went to bed in his room.

"What are you doing this weekend?" he asked.

"Nothing spectacular. Why?"

"I want to go away this weekend."

"Oh. Where do you want to go?"

"San Diego."

"Isn't that in California?"

"Yeah."

"Oh," I said.

"You don't want to?"

"That's just a far trip for the weekend."

"I just want to relax in a hotel room on the beach. Somewhere quiet with good Mexican good."

"Would it just be us two?" I asked.

"Of course."

"Then I'm in."

"We'll leave as soon as you get off work tomorrow."

I smiled. "I'm excited. I've never been to California."

"You'll love it," he said. He pulled up my shirt and kissed the skin of my stomach. "I love your body, baby."

"Thank you," I said. "I try to work out every day."

"It shows."

"And I have to stay thin for my job."

"I didn't realize that was a prerequisite."

"It's because it's a fashion magazine," I said as I rolled my eyes. "It's so stupid."

He pulled off my underwear and kept kissing me.

I went to grab my jersey but he kept it on. "No."

"Well, I want you to be naked."

He pulled off his shirts and boxers in a flash.

I chuckled lightly.

"I like making love without condoms," he said as he kissed my neck.

"It's nice, huh?"

"I really like it. I like coming inside you. That's the best part."

I ran my hands up his chest then felt his hard cock.

"Turn over," he said.

I did as he asked and felt his arm wrap around my waist. When he slid inside me, I moaned loudly. It didn't matter what position we did it in, it was always amazing. He leaned over me and pressed his lips against my ear, whispering to me quietly.

I felt him stretch me as he moved in and out. I still wore my jersey and his chest pressed against it while he bucked inside me. I held onto his headboard while he rocked me, making me scream. The neighbors probably heard me but I didn't care.

My body started to crumble. "Tony…"

"I'm there too, baby."

I clenched the wood. "Yeah…"

He breathed into my ear as we climaxed together, feeling the connection simultaneously. When I heard him moan, it heightened my arousal. Knowing he felt good made me feel good. He pulled out then lay on the bed. I collapsed on his chest, breathing hard.

"You're the best sex I've ever had," he said.

"I find that hard to believe."

"I already have you," he said. "Why would I tell you a line?"

"That's true."

He kissed my forehead. "It's so nice being myself around you. I don't have to hide anymore."

"I'm glad you don't." I started thinking about Janet. "I just wish—"

"Stop."

I fell silent.

"We aren't thinking about that anymore. We're happy. That's all that matters."

I sighed.

"I made you a few drawers to keep your stuff in."

"You did?" I asked with a smile.

"And there's a drawer in my bathroom so you can put your toothbrush and girly things away."

"Girly things?"

"You know, makeup, tampons…stuff like that."

I closed my eyes. "Orlando wants to go on a double date."

"Your friend from work?"

"Yeah."

"I'm down."

"He and his boyfriend want to check you out."

"I hope they don't fight over me," he said with a smile.

"I'll take them out if they try to steal my man."

"I don't know…I have my bet on the two gay guys. They'd probably beat you up."

"Hey, I work out!"

"They probably work out more than you do."

"Damn, you're right."

He buried his face in my neck. "So has anyone been bothering you?"

"What do you mean?"

"Like, Tyler or that piece of shit ex-boyfriend of yours."

"Oh," I said. "No."

"Good."

"Why would they?"

He kissed my neck gently. "If I lost you, I know I'd be doing everything in my power to win you back."

I rolled my eyes. "Danny doesn't stand a chance."

"I like hearing that."

I kissed him on the forehead. "No one stands a chance."

"Even better," he whispered.

"Are you making breakfast tomorrow?"

He smiled. "What would you like?"

"Pancakes and coffee."

"Okay," he said. "I'll make sure it happens. I have a Mickey Mouse pancake maker."

"You do?" I asked excitedly.

"I'm guessing you want me to use that one?"

"Duh!"

He laughed. "Stop being so adorable."

"I can't."

"I'm glad you can't." He cuddled next to me and closed his eyes.

I wasn't tired so I watched him sleep instead. He looked so peaceful and calm. Even though he lost his sister he seemed happier than he'd ever been. Now that he was honest with me, he seemed to be whole again. I couldn't lie and say I wasn't more attracted to him because he was loaded, because I was. But it wasn't about the money. Knowing he made his own empire by himself was truly amazing. He stood on his own two feet and made his own fortune. It was inspiring and amazing. And I loved everything about him. I felt like I won the lottery. I hated

that date with Tyler but I was so glad it happened. If it

hadn't, I wouldn't have walked into the bar and met Tony.

10

When I got off work on Friday, I was so excited for our trip. I couldn't sleep last night because I was too wired to rest. I went to my apartment and gathered my bags. Tony arrived a few moments later.

"Are you ready?" he asked.

"I can't wait!" I said as I clapped my hands together.

He smiled then kissed me. "We'll have a lot of fun."

A guy walked into the room and grabbed my suitcases. I flinched when I watched him.

"Don't worry. He's one of my guys," he said with a laugh. "He isn't robbing you."

"Oh," I said. "Okay. I was freaked out for a second there."

"Are you missing anything?"

"No," I said as I grabbed my purse. I opened it and handed him an envelope. "Here's my share for the trip. I think that should cover everything."

He stared at it then looked at me. "What are you doing?"

"Paying for my half of the trip."

Tony pushed it away. "I invited you."

"So?" I said. "I want to haul my own weight."

"Put that away," he said in a stern voice. His eyes narrowed and the angry side of him emerged. "I'm not taking it."

I sighed then returned it to my purse. "You don't have to pay for everything."

"I know," he said. "I'll let you pay for a dinner."

"That's it?"

"You're lucky I'm letting you do that."

I rolled my eyes.

He grabbed my ass. "What was that?"

I smiled. "Nothing…"

He kissed me hard on the mouth. "It didn't look like nothing."

"I'll do that again when we go to bed tonight."

His eyes darkened. "I knew you were kinky."

"A little."

We went to the limo on the sidewalk and got inside. I looked around in wonder.

"Have you never been in a limo before?"

I shook my head.

"Not even for prom?"

"I didn't go."

"Why not?"

"I didn't want to."

He held my hand as we drove to the airport. When we arrived, we went through a different customs aisle and boarded a small jet.

"Why are we on a small plane?"

"I own it," he said simply.

"Oh…"

We sat in the back and took our seats. After takeoff, we unbuckled our safety belts and relaxed. Tony sat in a lounge hair and wrapped his arm around my shoulder. I leaned against him and tried to process what was happening. I was on a private jet that my boyfriend owned. He had more money than I could ever imagine. It was unbelievable.

"Do your parents know about your fortune?"

"No," he said.

"So you don't tell anyone?"

"No. It isn't worth it. I tell people I work at a computer company. Something vague and boring."

"It seems like money is more of a curse than a blessing."

"It is most of the time. It hasn't been since I met you. It's nice being with someone that cares about me for who I am. I've always wanted to settle down and find a girl that I could spend my money on, giving her the world. It's just not meaningful when she's only there for that reason. Since you aren't like that, I have someone to spend my money with. It's a great feeling. I feel like I've been vindicated. I'm finally free."

"You don't need to spend money on me. Taking me to see the Rangers in the front row is already good enough."

He smiled. "You're happy with the little things in life."

"You know what I really like?"

"What?"

"When you get fresh popcorn at the movies. You know, the kind they just made with the butter on top."

"Sometimes you are so cute that I can't stand it."

I shrugged. "I grew up poor. You learned to love what you had and the one you were with."

His hands glided through my hair while he stared at me.

"Have you talked to Janet?" I asked.

"I told you not to bring her up."

"So we're just going to never speak of her?"

"Yep."

I looked away and stared at the plane.

After we landed, another limo drove us to a hotel on the beach. A few villas were alone the sand, private beach houses the led directly to the water. When we checked in, the bell boys moved our stuff in one of the villas.

"I can't believe we're staying here," I said.

"You'll love it."

There was a large balcony that overlooked the ocean, which contained a hottub. And the inside had a living room and a kitchen. Upstairs was the bedroom, which had its own balcony that overlooked the water.

After we got settled, we sat on the balcony and stared at the ocean. I watched the waves beat the shore for hours. I never grew tired of staring. The beaches in New York weren't the same. I stared at a family in the sand. A little boy was looking for crabs while his older sister built a sandcastle. When I looked at Tony, he was staring at me.

"You're beautiful." That was all he said.

I blushed.

"I find it really interesting that you're so humble about your looks. You are really gorgeous. I'm not just saying that because you're my girlfriend."

"Thank you...I'm just not used to the compliments."

"I find that unlikely. Men stare at you constantly."

"I don't notice," I said.

"You are such a hard find," he said. "A beautiful woman who doesn't know she's beautiful. You really are the perfect woman."

I blushed again.

"Have you ever considered modeling?"

"Now this has gone too far."

"Babe, I'm being serious."

"Shut up," I said playfully.

"I have connections in the industry. I could arrange something."

"No, thank you," I said. I considered asking him to find me another job as a fashion designer, one that I wouldn't hate. And I hoped by name dropping him my supervisor wouldn't disrespect me or treat me like Pia did. But I never asked because I didn't want to take advantage of him. I was with Tony because of who he was, not what he could offer me. And I never wanted him to question that.

"Let me know if you change your mind."

I stared at the ocean. "I could give you a private fashion show if you want."

"You have my attention."

"I packed something special."

"Ooh…tell me more."

"You'll have to wait until tonight."

"Damn," he said. "Now my mind will be running wild all day."

I stared at his face and suddenly realized something. "Why aren't you a playboy?"

"What?" he asked with a laugh.

"You have the money, the connections, the looks…why aren't you a permanent bachelor? You wouldn't have to worry about someone loving you for you and not your money."

He was quiet for a long time. "That got old really quick. It was fun in my younger years but now I want something more deep and meaningful. The single life isn't for me. I've been wanting to settle down for a long time but I never found a suitable partner. Having lots of sex with different girls is unfulfilling, and to be honest, totally depressing. With you, I feel like I have a best friend and a lover. I feel like I can tell you anything. And I know if I lost all my money tomorrow, you would still be right beside me. That's real. My money isn't. When I die, I can't take it with me. And you make me really happy. I think that some guys are meant to be bachelors and should never get married but I'm not one of them. When I see Beatriz and her family, I know that's what I want. When I see the way Janet looks at Scott, I realize I want a woman to look at me the same way. I don't know…I guess I'm just odd."

"I think you're really sweet. You keep saying I'm a rare find, but you're the diamond in the ruff, Tony."

He smiled. "That's the nicest thing anyone has ever said to me."

I reached for his hand and held it in my own. His thumb moved across my knuckles and touched me gently. We stared at each other for a long time, listening to the waves crash against the shore in the distance. A slight breeze ruffled my hair and took away the heat on the back of my neck. We stayed that way for a long time, neither one of us speaking.

When we went to dinner that night, we sat on the patio of the hotel. Candles shined bright on all the tables. I stared at Tony across from me, who met my gaze with a smile. He looked at the menu.

"What are you getting?" he asked.

"Too many choices. Do you have a suggestion?"

"I'll order for you," he said.

"Okay."

The waiter came and Tony made the selections. After our glasses of wine were poured, it was just us.

"Can I ask you some personal questions?" I asked.

He chuckled. "Baby, you can ask me anything that comes to mind."

"Wow…that's a lot of power."

"And I have a lot of trust for you."

"This opens up a new domain."

He smiled. "I have a feeling this is going to take a while."

"So, do you just bet on games that you choose or do you bet on all games?"

"Just the ones I want. I just call a guy and place my bet."

"Is there any strategy to it?"

"Well, sports are rigged. You have to get the inside scoop on most of the games."

"They are?" I asked incredulously.

He nodded. "But we gamble on a point spread so it's harder to win."

"How much money do you win?"

"It depends on how much each person put in."

"When you bet on the Rangers last month, how much did you win?" I asked.

"Almost a million."

"Holy gamoly!"

He laughed. "There's a few guys who won't participate in the bets because they think I'm cheating in some way."

"Are you?"

"It's impossible," he said. "I'm just very educated in sports."

"And smart."

He shrugged.

"What's the most you've ever lost?"

"Two million."

"That's insane," I said.

"It's a lot to take in."

"So, what do you do all day? Research?"

"No," he said. "I watch games all year round. I don't read books or anything like that. It's all about your instinct. On a typical day, I wake up and hit the gym for two hours, make a big breakfast, play video games, take a nap, then hang out with people when they get off work."

"Wow, you have it made."

He smiled. "I don't have any complaints."

"You play video games?"

"Yes," he said. "I'm a nerd."

"Why were you so hesitant to tell Janet everything? She seemed like she knew the truth, but not because you told her."

"Because I wasn't always doing things that were in accordance with the law," he said. "The less people who know, the better."

"Is it still illegal?"

"Sometimes it is. It's hard to explain. But since we only pay in cash, the IRS isn't too happy about it."

"Wow," I said. "It's like a whole new world."

"That's an understatement."

"Do you give your money away?"

"I give it to a few charities," he said. "And I hired an attorney to create a fake relative that passed away and left my parents a fortune of money. My dad lost his job and they were struggling to retire. I just did that and it solved the problem. Now they live comfortably."

"And they have no idea it was you?" I asked.

"Nope."

"Are you going to pay for Joey's college?"

"I was going to make up a fake scholarship he won," he said.

"I think Beatriz might figure it out."

"She's too stupid to figure it out."

I laughed loudly. "We need to stop ganging up on her."

"Why?" he said. "It's fun."

The waiter brought our food then walked away.

I dug into my pasta and enjoyed it. Tony had good taste in food and wine.

"What are you going to do with your kids?" I asked.

"What do you mean?"

"Are you going to tell them you have money?"

"No, probably not. If I do, they won't try to succeed in life, knowing they can rely on my money. I don't want that. My kids need to understand the value of a dollar and make a life for themselves."

I nodded. "That's probably for the best."

"But I will definitely give them everything they need to succeed."

"And awesome birthday parties."

He smiled. "Definitely."

When we were finished with our dinner, we walked back to our villa. As soon as we were inside, Tony stripped off his clothes and sat on the bed, completely naked.

"Right to the point?" I asked.

"I want my fashion show," he said as he leaned back on his elbows.

"You need to watch it naked?"

"I have a feeling I'm going to seduce one of the models."

"You're pretty cocky."

He winked. "You could say that."

"But my belly is big because I just ate."

He rolled his eyes. "No, it isn't. Now rock my world."

"You're so demanding."

"For you, I am."

"I'll be right back."

"Yes!"

I smiled as I walked away.

I went into the bathroom and changed into the teddy and garters. I put on black heels and placed a silk robe around my body. When I was done, I looked in the mirror. I fixed my blonde hair and adjusted my makeup. I definitely wasn't model material. I had no idea what Tony was talking about. I took a deep breath then walked out.

Tony stared at me while I approached the bed. His eyes already shined with desire. I turned around and untied my robe. It fell to the floor.

"Yowza," he said.

I ran my fingers through my hair then turned around.

His cock was already hard, leaning against his stomach.

I approached him then leaned over the bed, my tits hanging out of my bra.

Tony moaned quietly while he stared at me.

"Thank you for taking me here," I whispered.

He said something incoherent.

I leaned down and trailed kisses from his chest to his stomach. When I approached his crotch, he took a deep breath. I got to my knees then kissed the tip of his cock.

"Mmm…"

I licked the base to the tip then placed him in my mouth. He watched me the entire time, his breathing deep and shallow. When he thrust his hips gently, he started to crumble. Then he grabbed my face and pulled me away.

His lips were on mine as he guided me to the bed. He pulled off my bottoms and tossed them aside. "You look too beautiful for me not to make love to you."

My fingers dug into his hair as he inserted himself at my opening. He slid inside while he stared into my eyes, his hand resting on my neck. He moved deep inside, making me dig my nails into his skin. I opened my legs wider as he rocked into me, lighting me on fire.

The sweat started to drip down his back as he moved into me hard and fast. I rocked into him from below, wanting more than he could give. I was already coming, feeling my lower stomach light on fire.

"Tony, I love you."

He stopped for an instant, his eyes wide. After he recovered from the shock, he moved into me again. His face was pressed to mine as we moved together. "I love you, Cassie."

The explosion hit me, and I took him with me.

When we were done, everything was different. The words I said escaped my lips without any thought process. It just came out. But that's how I knew I meant them. There was no thought behind it. It was purely emotional. And that's how I knew it was real. I suspected I felt that way for a while, but I was too scared to say it. My erratic emotions pushed me off the cliff. And I was so glad Tony caught me.

His hands glided through my hair as he looked at me. He didn't pull out of me, staying connected to me. I stared into his eyes, seeing the unique green eyes that I adored. I didn't just see the beautiful colors, but I saw everything about him that I loved. I saw his good heart, his beautiful soul, his integrity, and his hopes and dreams. I knew how much he loved his sister, but he stood up for me when she was wrong. It would have been easy to turn his back on me and find someone else, but he didn't. He chose me. Only me.

'   Tony licked the sweat from my neck and chest. "Thank you for going on that horrible date."

I smiled. "I'm glad I did too."

"I owe Tyler a gift."

"Maybe an apology for threatening to rip his eyes out."

"Nah," he said. "I'm sure that threat keeps him away from you."

"How about a basket of mini muffins?"

He nodded. "Now we're thinking."

"I'll send one to his floor."

"What do you mean?"

"We work together."

His eyes widened. "I didn't fucking know that."

I rolled my eyes. "Calm down."

"No," he said. "He came to your apartment like a psychopath."

"He hasn't bothered me once."

"And he won't."

"Just let it go."

"I'll take care of him."

"What does that mean?" I asked. "You're going to threaten to kill him if he doesn't quit his job?"

"No, I'll pay him to quit his job and find something else."

"You're so crazy."

"You just told me you loved me," he said. "Everything is different now. I am fucking crazy. And I'm going to stay crazy."

"I never see him at work."

"That doesn't mean shit to me."

"We were just having a really beautiful moment but you ruined it by freaking out."

He rubbed his nose against mine. "We're going to have a lot more of those. Don't worry about it. I'll take care of Tyler."

"You don't need to worry about it."

"Are there any other men who work with you?"

"You aren't serious, right?"

"I'll just have someone investigate their company."

I grabbed a pillow and hit him in the head.

He laughed. "Two people can play this game." He grabbed one and hit me lightly on the leg. I wasn't gentle with him like he was with me. I smacked him hard. Tony didn't seem to be affected. He hit me again with his pillow but he was barely trying. It wasn't even a fair fight. I hit him again then felt myself be pinned down to the bed.

"You're getting a little carried away," he said with a smile.

"Well, you weren't fighting back."

"I'm not into hitting women. Not my style."

"It's a pillow stuffed with feathers."

"That doesn't mean anything," he said. "Janet gave Beatriz a black eye once."

"Good," I said.

He nodded. "That deserves another high-five." He let go of my hand and smacked my palm.

There was a knock on the door.

"Who is that?" I asked.

He looked at the time. "Cover yourself up," he said. He grabbed the robe from the ground and tossed it at me. He put on his jeans and opened the door.

"Here you are, sir."

"Thank you." He took the basket then closed the door.

"What if that was a girl?" I asked.

He raised an eyebrow. "What?"

"You're shirtless."

"So?"

"You're so sexist."

He took the basket outside.

"What is that?" I asked.

"Come and see."

I went outside and he started a fire in the stone fire pit. I looked in the basket. "Smores?"

"Yep."

"Ooh! I love smores."

He looked at me. "You get excited over little things. I like that."

"I'm easily pleased."

"I know that too," he said with a smile.

"That's because you're unbelievable in bed."

"Keep the compliments coming." He arranged the sticks and we sat in the chair, roasting our marshmallows. We made our smores and ate them together, getting our faces smothered in melted marshmallows and chocolate sauce.

"You got a little something right there," he said.

"Where?" I said, touching my face.

He kissed me and rubbed the chocolate on his mouth all over my face. "There," he said.

I laughed. "Gross!"

"You liked it."

I wiped my face with napkin then he wiped his. We roasted more marshmallows in the fire pit and watched the ocean in the darkness. No one was on the beach like we were the only people in the whole world. My heart didn't feel pained anymore. I was so worried I would never find anyone after what Danny did to me. And all the guys I dated were the scum of the earth. But then Tony fell from the sky, being a million times better than the perfect guy.

11

Our weekend was too short. We were back in New York Sunday night and I felt like we just left. I knew I should go to my apartment after spending all weekend with Tony, but I really didn't want to. I wanted to sleep in his bed with him, feeling him next to me. Sometimes he snored but it didn't bother me. Just knowing he was there was enough to keep my nightmares away.

The limo driver drove me to my apartment and Tony helped me carry my bags into my living room. When everything was settled he looked at me.

"Thank you for coming with me," he said. "I had a really good time."

"Me too," I said.

He kissed my forehead. "I'll see you later."

"Okay," I said quietly.

Tony stared at me. "What is it, baby?"

"Sleep with me."

"You want me to stay?"

I nodded.

"Then I'll stay."

"I'm sorry," I said. "I don't mean to be clingy. You don't have to stay."

He smiled. "No, it's okay. I wanted the same thing but I didn't want to scare you off."

"We're so cute."

"I'll tell Jack to take myself to my apartment."

"Okay."

He left and returned a few minutes later. We were both tired from the long flight so we fell into bed and went to sleep immediately. I had to work in the morning and I wanted to call in sick. But I was already in hot water so I knew I couldn't do a single thing wrong.

When I went to work the next morning, I saw Orlando.

"How was the weekend?" he asked. "Lots of sex?"

"I can barely sit down."

"Man, I wish I had that problem."

I smiled. "I'm sad it's over."

"I would be too."

"We dropped the L word."

He clapped. "That's fabulous."

"I'm very happy."

"Now we just need to get you engaged."

I laughed. "That's too soon."

"You wouldn't say no."

"Probably not."

"And isn't he a billionaire? Quit your job and eat Bon-Bons all day."

"I'm not with him for his money."

"That doesn't mean you can't take advantage of it."

"That isn't my style," I said.

"So, are we on for dinner tonight?" Orlando asked.

"Yep. Sushi."

"Stewart is excited."

"I hope you two can keep your hands to yourselves."

"We can, but you don't want to see that either."

I laughed. "You're horrible, Orlando."

Theresa knocked on my door. "Pia wants to see you, Cassie."

"Uh, thanks," I said.

She glared at me. "Now."

I stood up. "I'm coming."

Orlando's eyes widened. "Keep it cool," he whispered.

I followed Theresa down the hallway, my heart beating in my chest. I had never been called to Pia's office before, and since I had been struggling at work, I knew this conversation wouldn't be a good one.

When I reached her office, I waited outside until Theresa chauffeured me inside. She closed the door behind her and I took a seat in front of the desk.

Pia ignored me for about five minutes. She typed on her computer and checked the papers on her desk. I wasn't sure if I should say something. She knew I was there. There was no way she didn't see me.

"You wanted to speak to me, ma'am?" I asked.

She glared at me through her glasses. "Now you know how it feels to have your time wasted."

I knew this was going to be bad.

She continued to stare me down. "I've been very displeased with your performance. I have thousands of applicants for your job every day, but yet, I'm paying you to make utter rubbish for this magazine. It's a disgrace to this company and your colleagues."

I kept a straight face even though I felt like breaking down on the inside. There was nothing wrong with my work. I wasn't even sure what Pia wanted me to create. I really wished I had another job so I could just storm out and tell her to go to hell.

"Have you nothing to say?"

No, not really. "I'll do better next time."

"*You'll do better?* And what does that mean?"

"I won't let you down," I said calmly.

"Why do I have a hard time believing anything you say?"

If she weren't my boss, I'd punch her in the face. I seriously wanted to key her Mercedes in the parking garage. If there weren't any cameras, I'd probably get away with it. I didn't respond to her comment because I didn't have anything constructive to say. It sounded rhetorical anyway.

"Consider this your final warning. If your work is less than perfect, you'll be looking for another job. And believe me, I'll be bad mouthing you all over town. You won't find anything."

I kept my anger under control. "Anything else, ma'am?"

"Get out of my office."

I stood up and left. When I walked into my office, I shut the door and let the tears fall. I knew it was stupid to cry but I couldn't help it. The situation was totally unfair. I didn't do anything wrong. I knew my work was good. My models loved my gowns. Pia was the one who didn't understand fashion.

Orlando opened the door. "Oh my god. What happened?" He closed the door and came to me.

I told him everything.

He patted my back. "I'm so sorry, girl."

"I fucking hate her."

"You aren't the only one."

I wiped my tears away and controlled my breathing. "Are my gowns ugly, Orlando? Be honest."

"They are beautiful. I'm not just saying that."

"Then I don't understand."

Orlando shrugged. "I don't know. No one knows what she's looking for. I heard rumors that the management is lighting a fire under her ass to be the number one magazine in the country. Perhaps she's taking it out on everyone."

"Perhaps?" I said sarcastically.

"It'll be alright."

"No it won't," I said. "I need to start looking for another job now. It doesn't matter what I make. She won't like it. I bet tomorrow she'll have a bunch of candidates interviewing for my position."

"Worse case scenario, she fires you," Orlando said. "You'll find something else."

"She told me she would make sure I didn't get a job anywhere else."

"Wow," he said. "Pia is out for blood."

"Fucking bitch."

"Hey, we'll figure it out. I'll help you."

"Thank you, Orlando."

"I got your back, girl," he said. "Should we cancel dinner?"

"No," I said quickly. "I need a few laughs. Otherwise I'll go crazy."

"Okay. I need to get back to work."

"Okay." I stared out the window after he left, feeling my mind go blank. The first thing I wanted to do was call Tony and spill my heart out, but I didn't want to drown him in my work problems. And I didn't want him to do me any favors. Knowing him, he would offer.

After work, I got ready but told Tony not to come over for a few hours. I wanted him to, but I was still too upset to be around him. I would be nothing but a downer. I drank some wine and watched TV, trying to clear my head. When he finally came to my place, I felt a little better.

"Wow," he said when he walked inside, staring at me. "If your friends weren't gay, I'd be a little worried."

I was wearing a dress that made my breasts look perky. I tried to show off around Tony as much as possible. He always told me I looked nice and I liked hearing the compliments from him. "You look nice too."

"Nice?" he asked. "I give you wow, and I get nice?"

I laughed. "You look very fuckable."

"Ooh. I like that."

I wrapped my arms around him and hugged him for a long time, letting my stress wash away. He held me but said nothing. His strong arms made me feel better immediately. Everything was easier when I was with him. Nothing was complicated. I loved him with my whole heart and I knew he loved me in return. As long as we had that, we didn't need anything else.

He pulled away and kissed me on the forehead. "We should go."

"Yeah," I said.

We arrived at the restaurant and saw Orlando and Stewart already sitting at a table. When we walked over, Orlando jumped up and hugged me.

"You look hot, girl."

"Thanks," I said.

Stewart kissed me on the cheek. "It's nice to put a face to a name. Orlando talks about you all the time."

"I hope he says good things," I said.

"Mostly," Stewart teased.

I turned to Tony. "This is my boyfriend."

Their mouths both dropped.

Orlando nodded his head approvingly. "Very nice."

Stewart tried to get a peek of his ass. And he wasn't discreet about it.

Tony actually blushed. "It's lovely to meet you both."

"And it talks," Orlando said, mesmerized. He shook his hand.

Stewart shook his hand next. "Wow. You have big hands."

"Uh, thanks?' Tony said.

I laughed. "Let's sit down."

We took our seats.

Orland kept his hand on Stewart's thigh, and Stewart looked at the menu.

Tony placed his arm over my chair, his fingers touching my neck gently.

"Do you work out?" Stewart asked bluntly.

"Every morning," Tony answered.

"It shows," Stewart said.

"Why don't you work out more often?" Orlando asked.

"I do," he said offended. "I do Pilates."

"You aren't going to get muscles like that doing Pilates," Orlando said.

"Well, you don't work out," Stewart said.

"I work all day."

"I knew you were going to throw that in my face," Stewart said as he rolled his eyes.

Tony smiled, seeming amused. "How did you two meet?"

"At the Purple Cowboy," Orlando said.

"What's that? Tony asked.

"A gay bar," I said.

"Oh," Tony said. "Cool."

"And we've been in love ever since," Stewart said. "Even if that isn't always clear."

"What do you do at the magazine?" Tony asked Orlando.

"I'm in charge of jewelry and accessories. I find the top trending gems and incorporate them into our photo shoots. I have the best job ever," he said as he waved his hand.

Stewart looked at me. "I'm so sorry about your job. Orlando told me everything."

Tony looked at me. "What about your job?"

My eyes widened in alarm. I wasn't expecting this to come up.

Orlando shook his head. "Pia is a total bitch. I can't believe she fired you without actually firing you. She'll get what's coming to her."

Tony continued to stare at me. "What is he talking about, babe?"

Orlando looked frightened. "Whoops."

I avoided his gaze. "Nothing important."

"Did you get fired today?" he pressed.

I sighed. "It's a long story."

"And we have all night," he said.

Orlando took the reins. "I think Cassie makes gorgeous gowns. She's been doing it for years. And now Pia hates them. She gives her absolutely no feedback and keeps trashing them. So Cassie has one more chance before she gets sacked."

"Is that even legal?" Tony asked.

"Yes," I said quietly.

Tony gave me a sympathetic look. "You'll find another job."

"She basically said she would make sure that didn't happen," Orlando said. "That woman is a serial killer by night, I swear."

"That's totally uncalled for," Stewart said. "It's like she wants revenge."

I shrugged. "I don't know what her problem is."

Tony grabbed my hand. "Why didn't you tell me?"

"It just happened today," I said. "I didn't want to bring it up."

He leaned toward me and kissed me gently.

Stewart and Orlando both awed.

"I'll figure it out, baby," he said. "Don't worry about it."

"I'm fine, Tony."

"Quit tomorrow," he said. "I'll find you another job—a better job. In the meantime, I can take care of your bills."

"If only he was gay…" Orlando said.

"Tony, I really appreciate it, but I don't need your help. Thank you anyway."

He stared at me. "I don't want you going back there. You clearly aren't respected and treated right."

"Drop it," I said firmly.

"Why are you being so complicated right now?" Tony said. "I've found you a perfect solution. Why go back there where you are miserable? And I can make this woman's life miserable if I want to."

"Do it!" Orland said. "You would be the office hero."

I grabbed his arm. "Can we discuss this later?"

He stared me down. "Okay."

We got back to dinner and talk about other things. It was still tense because of the argument Tony and I just had. I really wished Stewart hadn't brought up the incident, but I couldn't be mad about it. I understood why he assumed Tony already knew. Any normal girlfriend would tell her boyfriend. Except most normal boyfriends weren't billionaires.

When we came back to my apartment, I prepared for the battle about to take place.

He stared at me. "Why didn't you tell me?"

"I'm so horny right now."

"What?"

I wrapped my arms around his neck and kissed him. "Make love to me."

He fell for my ploy but only for a second. "I know what you're doing."

"Trying to get laid."

"You're trying to avoid a fight."

I sighed.

"Why didn't you tell me?" he repeated.

"I didn't have a chance."

"You had three hours from when you left work until we went to dinner."

"I had errands to run."

He glared at me. "Be straight with me."

"I just didn't want to, okay?"

"Are you really going to lose your job?"

"I'm pretty sure I will."

He shook his head. "That's something you should tell me. I thought we were serious."

"We are," I said. "That has nothing to do with this."

"But it does. I love you. You love me. You should tell me everything, especially important stuff like this."

I crossed my arms over my chest and avoided his gaze.

"How long has this been going on?"

I shrugged. "Like a month."

"A month?"

"It's not a big deal."

"It is a big deal!" He came closer to me. "I want you to quit tomorrow. I'll take care of you."

"I don't want you to take care of me!"

"Too bad! And I'll find you another job if you want one. I can get you in with a better company, a better gig, with better pay. And I'll make sure your boss gets fired. Money fixes everything."

I glared at him. "Tony, I don't want your help. That's exactly why I didn't want you to know. I knew this is the response I would get."

He studied my face for a long time. "Why won't you let me help you?"

"Because I can figure it out on my own."

Tony didn't look convinced. "Babe, I know you aren't with me for my money. You don't need to prove anything to me. Please let me help you."

"No."

"You're being really annoying right now."

"So are you. Let me figure it out."

"Why?" he said. "You'll get fired and you'll frantically search for a job, not find anything because of this bitch, then take a job you don't even want and be screwed over. I'm opening a door for you. Now walk through it."

"No."

"What are you trying to prove?"

"I love you."

He sighed. "Babe, I already know that."

"But everyone is going to think that's what's going on."

"Who cares?"

"I do," I said. "I don't want there to be any doubt."

"Even if there wasn't, people would still assume. That's just how it is."

I shook my head. "I don't even want to work for a magazine again."

"What do you want? You don't have work at all if you don't want to."

"That will never happen."

"When we get married, it will."

"No," I said firmly.

"I could slap you right now."

I glared at him.

"What do you want, baby?"

"My boss hates my dresses but I know they are amazing. I just wished I had my own clothing line. She would beg to feature me and I could tell her to fuck off."

"Then make your own clothing line," he said simply.

"I've already tried," I said sadly. "I need a lot of money just to start up and there's no guarantee I would even be successful. I could lose everything."

"You would be if you had all the right connections and the right investors."

I looked at him. "Tony, no."

"Why not? It's an investment."

"You never would invest in something like that unless you were sleeping with me."

"I've slept with a lot of girls and I've never offered them shit. I'm in love with you. There's a big difference. And I'd appreciate it if you didn't forget it."

My eyes softened.

"Now take my offer."

Having my own fashion company was my dream. I had so many ideas. And I really thought I had the talent to be successful, despite what Pia thought. But I couldn't take the money from Tony. Janet would immediately assume I was using him. It was my dream to have this, but Tony was a different dream, a more important one. "No."

He marched to me then threw me on the couch, pinning mw down. "Yes."

I flinched at the anger on his face.

"You are doing this. We don't have to tell anyone."

"Tony, I love you so much."

"Baby, I know."

"I don't want to lose you."

"You can't," he said. "Not ever."

"I'm scared."

"Don't be," he said. "I can't let you fall and lose your potential. That would be hurt me a lot more than if you took this money then dumped me. Please do this for me."

"What if Janet finds out?"

"I don't give a shit if she does."

"I don't know…"

"I'm withholding sex unless you do this."

"What?"

"You heard me."

I chuckled. "That's just mean."

"I'm being serious."

"Can I think about it?"

"There's nothing to think about. You're marching in there and quitting your job tomorrow. You'll get your revenge when you become super successful. Then you'll tear her down. And I'll help."

I stared at him, still unsure what to do.

"I've made the decision for you. We're done here."

"Tony—"

"If you love me, you'll take the money."

"It's going to cost a lot."

He rolled his eyes. "You know how much money I made on the Yankee game today?"

I said nothing.

"A million. I think I can afford it."

"I'll pay you back," I said.

"I don't want your money, baby."

"I have to pay you back."

He sighed. "By then, what's yours will be mine anyway."

I felt my heart throb at his words. "I love you so much."

His eyes softened. "And I you."

12

I didn't quit my job the next day. Instead, I pretended that nothing was amiss. Tony wasn't very happy about it, but I was still debating what I should do. Even if I didn't tell anyone that Tony gave me the money to start my own company, people would connect the dots, especially Janet. But she hadn't called me in weeks. And even though I was livid with her, I missed her like crazy. And if I missed her, I knew Tony did too.

After work, I met Layla for a drink. I hadn't seen her in a while and I missed her. She was already sitting at a table, looking at her phone. I approached her then gave her a big hug.

She hugged me back. "Are you doing okay?"

I sighed as I sat across from her. "I've been better."

Layla pushed a drink closer to me. "I got your favorite."

I took a big drink. "Thanks."

209

A man approached our table then smiled at Layla. The creepiness was leaking out of him. I moved in my chair just to get away. He was eye-fucking the shit out of Layla.

"So, I was about to head out...."

Layla grabbed her drink and threw it in his face. "Fuck off."

He closed his eyes as the liquid dripped down his face.

I froze in my chair, unable to believe that actually happened.

After he slammed his fist against the table, he left the bar.

I stared at Layla. "What was that?"

"He hit on me earlier and he wouldn't back down. I just snapped."

"Kyle would be proud," I said.

"Kyle would take me on the table because he'd be so happy about it."

I laughed. "How is it with you two?"

"Good," she said with a smile. "I like having him around all the time."

"Work and at home," I said. "That's a lot of Kyle."

"And a lot of sex," she said with a wink.

"I'm jealous. I wish I worked with Tony."

"Believe me, we don't get a lot of work done."

"I can imagine," I said with a laugh.

"So, how is it with you and Tony? I haven't heard anything."

"It's great. I love him."

"Wow. That was quick."

"We've been together for two months," I said. "And you're one to talk. Didn't you drop the L word in the first month?"

She smiled. "Maybe…"

"That's what I thought."

"When did you sleep together?"

My cheeks blushed.

"You're such a whore," she said with a laugh. "On the first date?"

"The second."

"Oh," she said. "That's so much better."

"Sometimes I think I loved him the moment I met him. The connection was there immediately. And I hadn't gotten in laid in years. I was desperate and he delivered. And then I fell for him even more because he was such a sweetheart. If that was a mistake, it was the best one I ever made."

Layla stared at my face for a while. "You seem really happy."

"More than you'll ever know. We went to California a few weeks ago and it was so romantic. I just keep falling more and more. He keeps catching me so I just let go."

"He took you on a trip?"

"I don't want him for his money," I blurted.

Layla rolled her eyes. "Cassie, I know that. You don't need to tell me twice."

My eyes widened. "You believe me?"

"Of course I believe you. And besides, you didn't know he was rich until you slept with him, right?"

"Yeah."

"I feel like that's enough proof. And you wouldn't do that to Janet."

"I wish she thought the same."

She sighed. "I don't know what her problem is. I understand her hesitance, but this situation is just stupid. She shouldn't cut both of you out of her life."

I played with the coaster on the table and averted my gaze. "Did she say anything about me?"

Layla shook her head. "She never mentions you."

"Tony?"

"No."

"I hate this," I whispered. "I feel like a part of me is missing."

"I'm sure she feels the same way." The bartender brought her another drink and she sipped it. "What else is new with you?"

"I've been going through hell at work."

"What happened?"

"It's a long story," I said with a sigh. "Basically, I'm going to lose my job."

"What?"

I nodded. "It's out of my hands. I'm tired of fighting it."

"Are you looking for something else?"

I was quiet for a moment. "Tony said I should open up my own clothing line. I could be successful then get revenge on my old boss."

"That sounds like a good idea."

I looked at Layla. "It costs a lot of money."

"Get a loan."

"I could never get a loan big enough."

"Then what are you going to do?"

I was quiet.

"Oh…"

"I don't want Janet to think I'm taking his money because I'm using him. I'm not!"

"Now I understand."

"I don't know what to do. I really want to make this happen. I'll even pay him back. But I'm scared what other people will think. I can't lose Tony. He's the best thing that ever happened to me. I love him. I really do."

"I believe you," Layla said gently.

"Then what do I do?"

"Well, it doesn't sound like Janet is going to be changing her mind anytime soon. And she assumes you're using him anyway. If he offered, you should just take it."

"You really think so?"

"And you said you would pay him back, right?"

"Of   course."

"Then you should just do it," Layla said. "And Kyle and I can help. At Satin Magazine, we can order supplies for a discounted price."

"Thank you," I said.

"Of course."

I grabbed her hand across the table. "Thank you for believing me."

"You're my best friend," she said. "Of course I believe you."

I nodded then pulled away.

"So, this is exciting," she said with a smile. "You have to hook me up with some awesome clothes."

"Of course I will. If I'm ever successful with this."

"Tony's rich so he probably knows all the right people."

"I don't," I said. "He's just educated about sports. I don't see how he knows anyone in the business world."

She shrugged. "You never know."

After we had our drinks, I walked to Tony's apartment. I didn't tell him I was coming but I knew he wouldn't care if I stopped by. I missed him, like I always did, and I wanted to sleep with him. I always had a good night's rest when I was held in his arms.

When I knocked on the door, Scott answered.

"Hey," he said.

"What are you doing here?"

"Watching the game."

"Oh," I said. "I didn't know there was one on."

"There's always a game on." He opened the door wider.

When I came inside, I saw Tony sitting on the couch. He jumped up when he saw me. "Hey, baby." Tony picked me up, rubbing his nose against mine. "What a pleasant surprise."

"I didn't mean to interrupt. I didn't know you were having people over."

"You aren't interrupting anything," he said. "You can come over whenever you want."

"You shouldn't have said that," I said with a smile. "Now you won't be able to get rid of me."

"It's all part of my diabolical plan."

"I'll eat all your food, use all the hot water, and hog all the sheets."

His eyes brightened when he stared at my face. A slight smile was on his lips. "That doesn't sound so bad."

"You say that now…"

"I'll always say that." He put me down then opened a drawer in his kitchen. He pulled out a key then handed it to me. "Mi casa es su casa."

My eyes widened. "What?"

He wrapped his arms around me. "It's your key. Come over whenever you want."

"Uh, I can't accept this."

His happy expression turned dark. "You will take it. I didn't ask if you wanted it. I'm giving it to you."

"But this is your place."

"Exactly. And I can do what I want." He grabbed my purse and pulled my keys out. He clipped his onto the ring then returned it to my purse. "I never want to hear you knock again."

"What if you're doing something private and I just barge in on you?"

"I don't have anything to hide, baby."

"What if you're watching porn?"

He laughed. "I haven't watched porn since we got together. And I don't suspect I ever will again. I like the real thing."

"Well, I should give you my key too."

"No," he said quickly. "You don't have to reciprocate. I just want you to have my key."

I looked at it in my purse. It had the Rangers logo on it. So typical. "Well, thank you. That was very sweet."

He smiled. "That's what I wanted to hear."

"I'll let you get back to your game," I said as I moved toward the door.

"Whoa, hold on." He pulled me back. "Why did you come by?"

"Oh. Just to talk. But it can wait."

"Is everything okay?"

"Yeah."

He caught my saddened expression. "Let's go in my room."

"No," I said quickly. "Enjoy your game."

"Watching it isn't going to change the outcome of the score. I either win or I don't." He pulled me toward his bedroom then shut the door. "What's up?"

"I was hanging out with Layla."

"How did that go?" he asked as he sat on the bed.

I moved to the spot beside him. "I told her about the clothing line idea."

"What did she say?"

"She's supportive."

"And she doesn't think you're a gold digger?" he asked.

"No."

"She sounds like better friend than Janet."

I didn't have a response to that.

"So, that means we're really doing this."

"I'll pay you back."

He rolled his eyes. "If that makes you feel better about taking my money, then fine."

"It does."

"I'm glad you're pursuing this."

"Only if I don't lose you."

"You won't," he said as he held my hand.

"That's all that matters to me."

He caressed my knuckles with his thumb. "So, I have a few ideas to destroy your boss. My favorite idea is paying the company to fire her and ruin her reputation. Then, I'd pay every other major fashion company to not even interview her."

Even though I hated my boss, I didn't like that idea. "She has a family."

"So?" he snapped. "She threatened to do the same to you. I have a feeling she isn't bluffing."

"But…she's been working there for twenty years."

"Again, what's your point?"

"That's just…I can't do that."

He narrowed his eyes at me. "Are you being serious?"

"I can't do that to her."

"Even though she would do the same to you?"

"I just can't."

He sighed. "I think I just fell more in love with you, if that's possible."

"I'll get my revenge, but I won't do it like that."

"Well, I have another idea."

"Let's hear it."

The guys cheered when a score was made. Their voices carried into the bedroom.

Tony didn't seem to care. "Victoria Sullivan is a good friend of mine."

"The supermodel?" I asked incredulously.

He nodded. "I can have her come down to the studio and inspect your dresses. I'll ask her to like them and marvel at them, showing your boss that you are talented. But she'll wait until after your boss rejects your work. Then Victoria will make a big scene about it, saying your chief editor doesn't even know what the definition of fashion is. That will be a slap in the face."

My eyes lit up. "That would be awesome."

"I'll arrange it."

Victoria Sullivan was a household name. She had been in Sport Illustrated, was a Victoria's Secret model, and even had her own reality television show. She was a really big deal. I felt my heart clench painfully. "How do you know her?"

"All rich people know each other. We attend the same events and parties. Since we're only one percent of the country, there are very few of us."

I nodded. "But that didn't answer my question."

He squeezed my hand. "I've never slept with her, if that's what you're asking."

I breathed a sigh of relief.

He smiled. "Jealous?"

"Why wouldn't I be? She's a fucking supermodel."

"You're a fucking supermodel," he said.

I laughed.

He grabbed my face and looked at me. "I mean it. You could model your own clothes if you wanted to. I could ask Victoria to show you a few things."

"It's okay," I said. "I like fashion, not modeling. And I love food too much to be a model."

"Not all models have to be ridiculously skinny until the point they're anorexic. If you were in a lingerie ad, I can guarantee guys would jerk off to your picture."

That made me blush.

"I'll arrange everything with her."

"I'm really looking forward to this."

"I am too," he said. "And the revenge doesn't stop there. I'll make sure your clothes get recognized by the right people. Pia's magazine will be the only exclusion. I'm sure her superiors won't like that very much. They'll do the dirty work for us."

"Thank you for doing this for me," I said.

"You're welcome. I'm glad you're letting me help."

"I wouldn't if you had any doubt about my love for you."

"It's a good thing I don't."

I sighed when I thought about Janet. Now there was no going back.

Tony caught the look. "Don't think about her."

"I miss her."

"I miss her too."

13

When we met Victoria, I was immediately self-conscious. Models were usually Photoshoped so they looked totally different in real life. That wasn't the case with her. She was as beautiful and sexy as she was portrayed in every picture. She wore five inch heels and still walked gracefully. I would fall on my face. Her legs were long and lean and she had a tiny waist. Her breasts were perky and noticeable. I wondered if she had any work done.

When she approached Tony at the table, she leaned in and kissed him on the cheek. I didn't like that very much.

"How are you, darling?" she asked in a British accent.

"I'm well. How are you?"

"I'm doing better now." She smiled at him then flipped her brown hair over her shoulder.

"Vicki, this is my girlfriend, Cassie."

Vicki? He had a nickname for her? I kept a smile on my face and shook her hand. Her wrist was so small I could break it with my fingers.

Her smile seemed genuine but I couldn't be sure. "It's lovely to meet you."

"You too."

When we sat down, Victoria sat across from Tony. I immediately put my hand on his thigh, claiming him like a psycho. Tony didn't seem to mind. I knew it was unfair, but I already hated this girl. She stared at Tony like she was fascinated with his appearance.

"You look good," she said. "You're still diligent with your workout?"

"Every morning," he said with a nod. He didn't compliment her appearance, which I was grateful for.

"So, how are you? I've missed you."

I felt my anger rise. Tony said he didn't sleep with her but something obviously happened between them. He wouldn't lie to me, but I didn't think he was completely honest either.

"I've been busy with the team," he said. "It gets hectic during the season."

"Are they making it to the playoffs?" she asked.

"They better," he said with a laugh.

She sipped her water when the waitress came over.

I wasn't hungry at all. I just picked a random entrée from the menu.

Tony looked at me. "Babe, what are you getting?"

"Uh, the house salad."

He raised an eyebrow.

I had never ordered a salad when we went out together. I didn't even eat them at home.

He didn't press me and turned to the waiter. "I'll have the turkey sandwich, and she'll have the same."

"What?" I said.

Tony ignored me.

"And you, miss?" the waiter asked.

Victoria glanced at the menu. "I'll have the Santa Fe salad with no avocado, no cheese, and no dressing."

I almost rolled my eyes but I stopped myself.

The waiter nodded then walked away.

"So," Victoria asked. "What do I owe the pleasure?"

Tony placed his arm over the back of my chair. "I want to ask for a favor."

"I'd do anything for you, Tony."

I was hating her more and more.

He nodded. "Cassie works for Castle Magazine as a fashion designer."

Victoria looked at me. "Oh. I assumed you were a model."

I was speechless. "Uh…"

Tony smiled at me, clearly enjoying my embarrassment.

"No," I said.

"Have you considered it?" Victoria asked. "You have a nice complexion and perfect proportions. And the angles of your face are desirable."

"Are you being serious?" I blurted.

Victoria smiled. "Yes, dear."

Tony turned to Victoria. "She's so humble about her appearance, it borderlines complete ignorance."

"Well, you are very beautiful, Cassie," she said.

I turned the shade of a tomato.

"Anyway," Tony said. "She's having some problems with her chief editor. Basically, her boss continues to reject her work, and she's going to be terminated for it. We want some revenge."

"And how can I help?"

"Go into the studio and watch. When Pia disgraces Cassie, jump in and compliment Cassie's work. Then insult Pia. That's it."

She smiled. "Pia Giovanni?"

"You know her?" I asked.

"She's a bitch," Victoria said. "Yes, I know her. And I'll do it."

' "Thank you so much," I blurted.

"Absolutely," she said with a nod.

"I also wanted to talk to you about something else," Tony said.

"I'm listening," she said.

"Cassie is starting her own clothing business. She could use some help getting off the ground, marketing her work, shipping it to distributors, things like that. I would love it if you could lend her a hand. Of course, you can say no. There's absolutely no problem with that. I understand if you have other responsibilities and may have legal issues supporting Cassie's work."

Victoria was quiet. She ran her fingers through her hair then sipped her water.

"Take all the time you need," Tony said.

The waiter brought our food and set it down.

Victoria picked at her lettuce and I nibbled on my sandwich. I wished Tony had just ordered me the salad. I felt like pig when I looked at Victoria.

"I'll do it," she said. "After Cassie shows me her work. If I don't like it, I can't put my stamp of approval on it."

Tony nodded. "I completely understand. Thank you very much."

She nodded and ate half of her salad. I didn't understand how she functioned on such a small portion of food. I ate my entire sandwich because I was starving. All the fries were gone too. Tony still had some on his plate so ate those too.

Tony smiled at me as he watched, amused. "You're so cute."

I flinched at the compliment. Victoria must have heard him.

Tony placed his hand on the back of my neck and touched me gently. When his fingers brushed my hair, I shivered. His eyes shined bright with the love he had for me.

"You guys are cute," Victoria said.

"I think it's just her," Tony said. "How are you and Fernan?"

"Good," she said. "He's in Italy until next week. I've been a bit lonely."

"I'm sorry," Tony said.

She sighed. "I'll manage."

After Tony paid for lunch, we went to the sidewalk. He embraced Victoria then pulled away. She kissed him on the cheek then smiled at him. Even though she was seeing someone, I didn't like it when she kissed my boyfriend. I kept a straight face since she was doing me a huge favor. Victoria hugged me next then kissed me on the cheek. I realized the affection might be a cultural practice. She was from England. Maybe I completely misread that.

"I'll see you tomorrow," she said.

Tony nodded. "Thank you, Vicki."

"Anything for you." She got into a cab and drove away.

Tony put his arm around my waist then held me close. "It looks like our plan is in motion."

"Yeah."

He stared into my face. "What?"

"Nothing…"

Tony sighed. "There's no reason to be jealous."

"I'm not."

"I can see it on your face."

"Well, you lied to me."

His eyes narrowed. "Excuse me?"

"There was something between you."

He looked away and watched the people go by. His hand fell from my waist then moved into his pocket. "We dated."

"So you lied to me?" I felt my anger explode. After Danny lied and cheated on me, I had absolutely no tolerance for that.

"No," he snapped. "I'm not a liar. I've never been one nor will I ever be."

"Then what happened?"

"We dated for a few weeks. She and I fooled around but we never went that far."

I wasn't sure what to say. I didn't like the idea of him kissing her, but it was better than him sleeping with her. "Why did you break up?"

He sighed. "I think Victoria is an amazing woman. She built the empire she has now, starting with absolutely nothing. But she and I just didn't...hit it off. She's very superficial and shallow. I knew she wasn't with me for my money because she's richer than I am, but I didn't feel anything for her. I thought I would fall for her but it never happened. So I ended it before she got hurt. And I'm glad I did it because she and I are still friends. There's nothing more to the story."

"You intentionally misled me."

"No, I didn't," he said. "But I didn't want you to miss this opportunity because of something so petty."

"Petty?"

"Yes, petty," he snapped. "I love you. I haven't loved something like this in a really long time. The last person who had my heart broke it years ago. So, there's nothing to feel threatened by. I could have her whenever I wanted her, but I don't. It's just you."

I avoided his gaze and looked at the street. I knew I was being immature but I couldn't help it. It didn't bother me that he dated her. It bothered me that he downplayed their relationship. "Danny cheated on me and lied to me for months. I'm very susceptible to lying. It's something I don't tolerate."

"And I didn't lie."

"You still stretched the truth. I don't accept that behavior."

He sighed. "Cassie, I'm sorry. I won't do it again. But I doubt you want to hear about every girl I've dated or fucked. I'm just trying to protect your heart. I know I wouldn't want to hear about it if the situation was reversed."

"The truth is still better."

Tony wrapped his arms around me and looked into my face. "You can trust me, Cassie. I don't want you to ever feel like you can't. I made a mistake and I won't repeat it. I'll always be blatantly honest with you. If that's what you want."

"One more chance."

He nodded. "I won't let you down."

"Thank you."

He kissed my forehead then ran his fingers through my hair. "I really hope this doesn't change our plan. Victoria's help is essential in both places. If you have her support for your company, your clothes will be sold everywhere. Magazines will want to interview you. And I bet Victoria would even model for you if she likes your style. Please don't let your jealousy interfere with that."

"It's not the jealousy that bothers me."

"Then don't let my stupidity ruin it."

I took a deep breath. "Okay."

"Now let's go home."

We went back to his apartment and watched TV on the couch. I curled up next to him and enjoyed the scent of his skin. His fingers ran through my hair and touched the back of my neck.

"The guys are coming over."

"Is a game coming on?" I asked.

"Yep."

"I'll get out of your hair," I said as I moved away.

He grabbed me. "Just because I'm watching a game doesn't mean you have to leave. You're always welcome here."

"I don't want to intrude."

He stared at my face. "Did Danny do that?"

I wasn't expecting the question. I didn't like talking about him. "Yeah."

"Well, I'm not him. I like it when you're here. You don't need to leave."

I smiled. "Okay. I just didn't want to cramp your style."

He raised an eyebrow. "Having my ridiculously gorgeous girlfriend sit on my lap while I watch the game isn't cramping my style, baby. It's a little uncomfortable because I have a hard on all the time, but that's it."

I blushed.

The guys came over an hour later. The TV was turned up and the pizza arrived. I sat on Tony's lap while he watched the game then went into the kitchen when I wanted another beer. Scott came beside him.

"How are you?" he asked.

I hated looking at him. He always reminded me of Janet. "I'm okay."

He nodded. "Just so you know, Tony's birthday is this week."

"It is? He didn't tell me."

"Janet said he's always really quiet about it. I figured he didn't tell you."

"Well, thank you for letting me know."

"Of course."

"Does Janet talk about me?"

He shook his head.

"What about Tony?"

"She says she misses him like crazy."

"She hasn't thought about talking to him?" I asked.

"No," he said. "She's sticking to her guns. She really doesn't want you two together."

I sighed. "I hate this."

"I know," he said as he patted my back.

"I hate not seeing my best friend. But I hate Tony not seeing his sister more."

"It's a crappy situation."

I stared at Tony while he watched the game. He didn't talk about Janet but I knew he was upset about the situation. He and Janet were close, as close as she and I were. I was breaking up a family by staying with him. It was unfair and I didn't do anything wrong, but I still felt responsible. The more I thought about it, the more depressed I became.

14

My heart was racing all morning. It was my time to shine and I was nervous about taking the spotlight. I worked really hard to perfect the dresses I designed. I stopped trying to figure out what Pia wanted and just created something I thought was beautiful. I was quitting whether Pia like it or not, so I didn't bother trying to impress her.

Orlando kept moving around, unable to stand still. "This is going to be epic. I'm putting my phone on the table so I can record everything."

"Don't," I said quickly.

"Why? I have to broadcast it."

"She's going to know it was you."

"Who cares? Hopefully you get her fried."

"Well, that won't happen overnight," I said.

"The video might help," he said mischievously.

I glared at him.

"Cassie, you live in a catty world. As a woman, you have to scratch, hiss and bite. That's how you survive."

"I'm above that."

Gloria and Winnie came out wearing the dresses I created. The dark purple looked great on Gloria and the blushing pink complemented Winnie perfectly.

"These are my favorite," Gloria said. "Pia will love these."

I laughed. "I find that unlikely."

Gloria spun in a circle. "It's so light but elegant at the same time."

"It's all about the material," I said. "And it holds the color. You could wash it twenty times before it started it fade."

"You should make clothes for a living," Winnie said. "Not just for a magazine."

I kept my secret. I didn't want anyone to know.

Victoria came inside, making everyone turn their head.

"OMG!" Orland hopped on his toes. "It's Victoria Sullivan!"

"Hello," she said as she shook his hand. "It's lovely to meet you."

"I love you," he blurted.

She chuckled. "That's always nice to hear."

Gloria's jaw dropped. "What the…"

Winnie looked just as shocked.

Victoria hugged me and kissed me on each cheek. "How are you, darling?"

"I'm well," I said. "How are you?"

"I'm excited to be here," she said. She took a seat in the chair and Orlando handed her a glass of champagne.

Gloria leaned toward me. "How do you know her?"

I shrugged. "We just ran into each other."

Gloria still looked shocked.

I never felt popular or cool my entire life, but I definitely felt like a badass in that moment. Winnie and Gloria were looking at me with new eyes. I hoped Pia would have the same reaction.

Orlando looked down the hallway. "The witch is coming."

"Good luck," Gloria said.

"There's not enough in the world," I said.

Pia strutted in, wearing an elegant suit with tall heels. Her hair was slicked back and she wore golden hoop earrings. Her assistant stood by her side, trying to anticipate her every move. I felt bad for her. I would kill myself if I had to be bossed around by Pia every day.

Pia walked around Gloria then sighed.

I knew what that meant.

She walked to Winnie and did the same thing. Her face was unreadable, but I could tell she was disappointed with my work—again.

I didn't care at this point. I knew I understood fashion better than most people. My work wasn't garbage. Pia was the only person who didn't care for it. Her opinion meant less than nothing to me.

"No," she said.

I said nothing, crossing my arms over my chest.

"You can pack your things," she said simply.

Victoria stood up then grabbed the dress Gloria was wearing. "Did you make this?" she asked incredulously, looking at me.

"I did."

"Everything?"

"From the drawing to the manufacturing."

Pia narrowed her eyes at Victoria. A glimmer of recognition flashed across her irises. I wondered what she was thinking.

"They're amazing," Victoria said. "I love the color."

"Thank you," I said.

She went to Winnie then examined the dress. "This would sell on my show, not to mention everywhere else. This is nothing less than fabulous." She turned to Pia, scorn in her gaze. "How do you not recognize a masterpiece when you see it?"

Pia didn't react, but I knew she was livid.

"I want these dresses," Victoria said. "But I want a lot more of them." She walked around then returned to my side. "You're a fashion genius, Cassie. I'm very glad I met you today. You're exactly what I'm looking for."

Pia took a step forward. "Cassie's creations are owned by Castle Magazine. They are not allowed to be taken and sold by other distributors. To do so would be unlawful."

"But you just fired me," I snapped.

Pia shifted her weight. "No, I didn't."

"You told her to pack up her things," Victoria said.

Pia looked at her assistant, demanding her to resolve the situation.

She stepped forward and opened her mouth.

"Do not insult me by making me speak to a pawn," Victoria snapped. "You just excused Cassie from her employment. We all heard it. She's working for me now."

"She isn't going anywhere," Pia said.

"I thought you said I was creating garbage?" I said.

Pia held my gaze but didn't speak.

"And I quit anyway. This place is a joke," I said. "And I'm taking my designs with me. Good luck finding my replacement."

Pia put her hand on her hip then turned to her assistant. "Take care of this." She left the room and disappeared.

Theresa came to me. "On behalf of Pia, I apologize—"

I held up my hand. "I'm leaving. Nothing you say will change that."

Her eyes widened in panic. "Cassie, please stay. I already screwed up once. If I do it again, she'll fire me. I have to get you to stay."

"I'm sorry," I said.

"Please," she said. "I have a little boy."

I sighed. "Do you want to work for me?"

"Doing what?" she asked.

"I need an assistant."

"Are you being serious?" she asked.

"Do you want it?"

"What are you doing?"

"I'm starting my own company," I said. "I'm sick of this place."

She smiled. "I'm sick of this place too."

"Then you're hired."

"Yes! Pia is my worst nightmare. I only took this job so I could get into the photography department."

"Well, now you can quit."

"Excuse me," Orlando said. "Shouldn't I be offered a job first as your best friend?"

I smiled. "What do you want to do?"

"Jewelry and accessories—duh."

"You're hired."

Victoria nodded her head in approval. "It looks like you got your crew."

"Thank you for everything," I said.

"And it's not over. I really do love your work. I'd be happy to help you in any way that I can."

"Really?"

She nodded.

I hugged her. "Thank you."

"Of course," she said as she patted me on the back.

"Let's pack up our stuff and get the hell out of here," Orlando said.

"Let's do it," I said. I went into my office and packed my stuff, dumping it into a box. Victoria walked inside.

"I wanted to give you this before I go." She handed me an envelope with Tony's name on it. "Can you give this to him on his birthday?"

I took it with shaky hands. "Sure."

"Thank you." She turned and left.

I stared at the envelope for a long time. My mind was working in overdrive. When I felt the paper in my hands, I could distinguish the note inside. It wasn't a birthday card. I held it up to the light and saw the feminine writing. I couldn't make it out.

"What are you doing?" Orlando asked when we walked in.

"Victoria wants me to give this to Tony."

He raised an eyebrow. "That's weird."

"She said it's for his birthday."

"So why are you trying to read it?"

I averted my gaze. "They used to date."

"Oh…now you want to know what it says?"

I nodded.

"Well, I don't think Victoria would help you then give you a love note to give to Tony, especially if it contained anything inappropriate. That wouldn't make any sense."

I sighed. "You're probably right."

He crossed his arms over his chest. "Then why do you still look like that?"

"I don't know…I guess Danny screwed me up more than I thought."

"You're just being paranoid," he said.

"I just want to know what it says."

"And what difference would that make?"

"I don't know…"

"Well, open it and read it. Put it in a different envelope and he'll never know."

I felt the guilt rise. "That would be wrong."

"Then just give it to him."

"But what if it says something bad?"

"Like what?" he asked.

"Like she wants to give them another try or something…"

Orlando stared at me. "If you're that paranoid about it, just read it. I'm sure it doesn't say anything like that."

"Really?"

He nodded. "It wouldn't make any sense for her to give it to you if she did."

"You're right."

"So open it and read it. You'll feel better."

I opened it and took out the paper.

Darling,

Seeing you with Cassie leaves me feeling weak and confused. You're so sweet to her, gentle with her. It makes me wonder how it would feel to be the object of your affection, the woman in your heart. And, I think I could be the woman in your heart. When we broke up, I felt broken and destitute. I would really love another chance. I thought I loved Fernan, but being around you makes me realize I don't. I would really love to have another go at things. And I think you won't be disappointed.

If you don't feel the same way and I just crossed a line, please disregard this message and never speak of it again. I would rather settle as your friend than lose you entirely.

Love, Vicki.

My hands were shaking.

Orlando's eyes widened. "That doesn't look good." He took it and read it. "Wow."

"What do I do?" I whispered.

"Don't give it to him, obviously."

"Really?"

"It's just going to mess with his head. And she even said she didn't want to speak of it again. She would never know that you didn't give it to him."

I felt sick to my stomach. "I can't believe she would do that."

"I doubt it's personal, Cassie."

"Why is she helping me if she wants Tony?"

"That's a very good question," he said. "And I don't know the answer."

I took the letter and dropped it on my desk.

"Don't give it to him," Orlando said. "He's better off not knowing."

"But that's wrong…"

"He'll never know."

"I guess." I still felt apprehensive about it.

"Victoria is out to get your man," Orlando said. "You can end it now by destroying that letter. She'll give up because she'll realize he isn't interested. And all of this can go away."

"I love him."

"Then fight for him."

"I—I can't do it."

Orlando snatched the letter then threw it in the shredder.

"Orlando!"

"I'm helping you, Cassie."

I opened the lid and saw the shredded remains. It was totally destroyed.

"Now just forget about it," he said.

"I'll just tell him the truth."

He shook his head. "I wouldn't advise that. How would you know what the letter said unless you opened it?"

"Damn…"

"The damage has been done, Cassie."

16

"I contacted my lawyer and got all the patents and licenses taken care of," Tony said as he sat in his office, going over the paperwork. "And I found an offshore manufacturer to produce the clothes at minimal cost."

My heart skipped a beat. "Where third world civilians work for fifty cents a day?"

Tony shrugged. "That's what my business friends suggested. They produce high amounts of product in little time."

"No."

He stared at me, waiting for me to elaborate.

"We manufacture only in the United States. It will create new jobs and will protect innocent people from being forced into servitude."

Tony nodded. "It will cost you more. I don't care how much you want to spend. I can afford it. But if you really intend to pay me back, it'll take you much longer."

"That's fine."

He smiled. "You're amazing."

"I'm a humane person."

"And we need more business owners like that." He opened a file. "I'll let them know that we'll on stay on American soil. I'm sure we'll find something. In the meantime, Victoria is taking your clothes and modeling them. They've already gotten a lot of attention. And when she said they weren't available, people only became more interested, naturally."

The mention of Victoria made me sick. I knew I should tell him the truth. What I did was wrong and inexcusable. "Tony…"

"Yes, babe?"

"About Victoria…"

"What?" He looked at me with the beautiful green eyes I adored. I didn't want to lose him. He was everything to me. Nothing good would come from this secret. I chickened out. "She's been really helpful."

He smiled. "I'm glad. She's a very nice person."

I couldn't disagree more.

He opened his checkbook. "The supplies, licenses, everything has been paid for. I've opened an account in your name and transferred the rest of the funds to it."

"An account?"

"Yeah," he said. "That way you can control everything and not ask me for money every time you need it."

I was speechless.

He handed me the envelope. "All the information is in there."

I opened it and saw the amount. "Tony…this is too much."

"Believe me, it's not. You may need more."

"But everything has already been paid for, the advertising, the marketing, the supplies…what's this for?"

"You'll need to pay your salary along with the rest of your workers, plus gas and electricity at your studio downtown."

"I don't think I need twenty million for that."

"That's my investment," he said. "If you don't use it, then just leave it there."

My hands shook. "I—are you sure?"

He smiled at me. "I'm more than sure. Now chase your dream."

"I couldn't have done this without you."

"I'm glad I could help, baby."

"You're so good to me. I—I don't deserve it."

"That's completely untrue," he said. He came around the desk then sat beside me, pulling me into his lap. "I am the one who doesn't deserve you."

My heart ached at his words. I always assumed I would end up alone or with an average guy. I never expected to win the lottery like this, getting the most amazing guy in the world. "I want to take you out to dinner tomorrow."

His eyes widened for a second before he adopted a stoic expression. "And wht is that?"

"To celebrate your birthday."

He sighed. "How'd you know?"

"Scott."

"That bastard."

"Why don't you want to celebrate your birthday?"

"I just don't."

I ran my fingers through his hair. "I would like to do something for you."

"You know what I want?"

"Hmm?"

"To not acknowledge it at all."

I thought that was odd. "Why?"

"Drop it, please."

I stilled at the annoyance in his voice. "Can I still cook you dinner?"

"I guess."

I kissed his forehead. I hated seeing the pain in his eyes. There was something more to this story. I wished he would confide it in me.

Tony was in a bad mood for the rest of the night. We watched TV in the living room then went to bed. We normally made love or fucked like animals, but Tony just lied there. I sensed the hostility radiating through him so I stayed on my side of the bed and didn't touch him. I had never felt more distant with him.

The next morning, I went to work at my new studio. Orlando and Theresa were already there, their excitement bubbling. The studio was cluttered with fabrics and supplies. We hadn't had the time to organize anything.

Theresa and Orlando did most of that while I got to work, creating new designs that Victoria could feature for me. I kept thinking about what I should get Tony for his birthday but I couldn't conjure an idea. What did you buy someone who already had everything? I decided to make him something instead.

I took a thick fabric from the bottom of a box and made a scarf. It contained the colors of the Rangers, the logo right across the middle. Tony didn't seem like someone who wore scarfs, even in the chilling winter of New York, but I knew he would appreciate it. He might wear it to the games if I was there.

When my workday was over, I bought groceries and cooked dinner. His gift was placed in an unadorned box on the table. I made lasagna because I knew it was his favorite. It drifted across the apartment and filled my nose with the smell of oregano and garlic.

He came over fifteen minutes late, which was unusual for him. He was always punctual.

"Hey," I said as I kissed him.

"Hey." His kiss was weak.

I didn't acknowledge his birthday like he asked, but I could still sense the depression in his body. I felt like he didn't even want to be there. He turned on the TV and watched a college game. Normally he offered to help in the kitchen. Today, he was in another world.

"What did you do today?" I asked.

"Nothing interesting," he said plainly. "You?"

"I worked."

"How are you liking it?"

"I love it. It's weird to be your own boss."

He nodded. "It's the best."

I set the table. "Come eat."

He turned off the TV and sat across from me. "It smells good."

"I hope it tastes good too."

We ate quietly. The box sat in the middle of the table. Tony didn't look at it or question it. He ate two servings and demolished the garlic bread. I assumed that meant he enjoyed it. When he was done, I slid the box toward him. "I got this for you."

He glared at me. "What did I say?"

"You told me not to acknowledge your birthday. I'm not. I just found something I thought you'd like."

He didn't grab it.

"Tony, please."

He sighed then opened it. When he held up the scarf, he stared at it for a long time. "Did you make this?"

I nodded.

A small smile stretched his lips. "That was—very sweet."

"I hope you like it."

"I love it." He turned his gaze onto me, his eyes a little brighter than they were before. He rose from his chair then kissed me on the lips. "Thank you."

"You're welcome."

"I'll wear it to every game." He returned it to the box and placed it on the table.

I cleaned up the dishes and he tried to help me.

"No," I said. "Go sit down."

He didn't argue with me and went into the living room.

After I was done, I sat beside him. "Is there anything you'd like to do?"

"No."

His sour mood had returned.

"Tony, why are you acting like this?"

He sighed. "I don't want to talk about it."

"Now or ever?"

"Ever."

I rubbed his arm. "I thought we told each other everything."

He turned off the TV and tossed the remote on the couch. "Every year, my sister cooks me dinner. Mom, Dad, and Beatriz and Hank come over and we spend the evening playing board games and talking. It's been a tradition since I can remember."

I felt my heart fall. "I'm so sorry."

Tony was silent.

"Did she call?"

"No."

I rubbed his arm, not sure what to do.

"I miss her," he whispered. "I miss my family."

I forced the words from my mouth. "We can break up and—"

"No."

I stared at his face.

"Janet is wrong. She needs to realize that and apologize."

"But you—"

"No," he said. "I won't change my mind. But that doesn't mean this isn't difficult for me. I pick on my sister but she's my closest friend. I tell her everything. I've wanted to talk to her so much this past month, tell her what's going on in my life. You don't realize how much you need someone until they are gone. Scott gives me reports about her, but it isn't the same. I haven't heard from her once. It's like she disappeared."

This was killing me. I hated being separated from Janet, but seeing Tony this miserable over it just made me feel worse. I felt like I was breaking up a family. This was all my fault. If I wasn't selfish, I would just end the relationship. Family was more important than I was. But no, I was a very selfish person, caring more about keeping my boyfriend than doing what was right for him.

His phone rang in his pocket but he didn't answer it. Instead, he stared at the blank screen. When it rang again, he sighed. He dug it from his pocket and looked at the screen. It was Victoria. He answered it.

"Hello?" He paused for a moment, listening to her speak. "Thank you."

I assumed she called to wish him Happy Birthday. A text message would suffice. She didn't need to call him. I really hated her. She wanted to keep Tony all to herself. I didn't understand why she was helping with my career or why she gave me that letter, trusting me implicitly, but I knew there was a reason.

"What letter?"

Fuck.

"No, Cassie didn't give me anything."

This was going to be bad.

"I'll talk to her." He hung up.

My heart was beating so fast I thought it would stop. I was caught red-handed.

"Cassie, Victoria just told me she gave you a letter a couple of days ago. Why didn't you give it to me?"

"Uh, I forgot."

"Well, can I have it now?"

I was cornered. There was no way out. "Tony, I—I don't have it."

His eyes narrowed. "Why not?"

"Because it was shredded."

"I'm not following," he said. "Why did you destroy something she wanted me to have?"

"Because she wants to get back together with you."

Tony stared at me, his eyes starting to turn dark. "How do you know this?"

"I read it…"

He stood up and paced around the room. "So, she gave you a letter to give to me, and you decided to open it, read it, and then destroy it without telling me?"

I avoided his look.

"Answer me."

"I—I was just scared that she wanted to get back together with you."

"What does it matter?" he snapped. "That's not an excuse. I can't believe you would go through my stuff like that. And you had no right to destroy it!"

"I'm sorry! Orlando is the one who shredded it. I was going to give it to you but he took it away."

"You still could have told me," he said.

"I tried, but…I was scared how you'd react."

"And you really thought it would be better if I found out like this?"

"In the letter she said she would never mention it again."

His eyes shined with anger. "So you were never going to tell me? Wow."

"I'm sorry! I just didn't want to lose you."

"How can you not trust me?" he snapped. "I told you I loved you. I gave you thirty million dollars! What the hell is wrong with you?"

"Danny...I just don't want to go through that again."

He kicked my coffee table on its side. Everything on the surface crashed to the ground. "Is that supposed to justify it? I'm sorry that your ex cheated on you, I really am, but how dare you assume that I would do the same." He shook his head, clenching his fists. "This is unacceptable."

"I'm sorry..."

"You said that already."

"I mean it."

"Fuck you, Cassie. You were pissed when I lied to you, even though I didn't, and you did the same thing but a million times worse. You're a fucking hypocrite."

I felt my eyes water. I blinked my eyes so the tears wouldn't fall.

"Now I don't trust you."

"I love you so much," I whispered. "I just didn't want to lose you."

"I ended the relationship with Victoria because I didn't love her. Why would I go back to her? That makes no fucking sense. You just dug your own grave, Cassie."

My heart clenched painfully. "What does that mean…?"

He stared at the ground, putting his hands on his hips.

"Tony?"

He still didn't speak.

"Please don't leave me."

Tony walked to the door then opened it.

"Wait! Please don't go."

"I need space right now." He didn't turn around.

I was growing desperate. I didn't want him to leave. When I thought about Victoria, my brain started to hurt. Why did she ask him about the letter if she said she wouldn't? None of it made sense. Then it hit me. "I know what she's doing."

He turned around. "What?"

"Victoria planned all of this so you'd break up with me. Then she would slide in and pick up the pieces."

He shook his head. "You're fucking unbelievable."

"Why would she help me if she wanted to get back together with you? It doesn't make sense. Why would she give me the letter that proclaimed her love for you? She did all of this to make herself look good and me look bad."

He crossed his arms over his chest. "Even if that was true, no one forced you to open that letter, Cassie. I don't care what Victoria does. As long as she doesn't touch me or make a move, I will always be civil to her. If she made a trap, you're the one who walked right into it. This is the bottom line; none of this would have happened if you trusted me."

"I do trust you."

"Don't lie to me!"

"I do," I said. "I just let my past get to me."

His eyes burned with anger. "How can I ever trust you?"

"You can," I said. "I'll never do something like that again."

"Have you been going through my phone too?"

"Of course not!"

He shook his head.

"Babe, I'm so sorry. I love you. Please don't go."

"I'm so fucking pissed right now."

"Please don't break up with me." The tears fell down my face. I started to sob, hating the idea of losing him. I couldn't go on if he left.

He gave me a sympathetic look. Tony came to me and wrapped his arms around me. "You still don't trust me."

I sobbed into his shoulder. "What?"

"I'm not leaving you. I'm hurt you think I would."

"But—I was wrong."

He sighed. "I'm really pissed at you right now, Cassie. I can't say that I'm not. But we'll work through it."

I gripped him tightly. "Thank you."

Tony pulled away. "I should go."

"Please stay."

"I haven't been this angry in a long time, Cassie. I just want to be alone."

"But it's your birthday."

"And it's the worst birthday of my life." He walked

out and slammed the door.

Tony didn't call me for the next two days. He said we would work through our relationship so I gave him the space he needed. I really regretted what I did. It was stupid and selfish. If I had just told the truth, that I read the letter, he probably wouldn't be nearly as angry. After everything I did, I'm surprised he didn't dump me. If the situation was reversed, I know that's what I would have done.

I went to work and completed my designs. They were shipped out to models and designers Tony knew, where they were showcased at different distributors. Almost immediately, I got invoices requesting more of the gowns I was creating. I sent them over to the manufacturer and cashed the check. It was too good to be true. My business had taken off almost immediately. If it weren't for Tony's connections, it would have taken me a decade to get to the level I was now, if it ever became successful at all.

Magazines wanted to feature me and have interviews. I almost fainted when I got my first one. After they rolled in, I received one from Castle Magazine. Rejecting that request gave me the greatest satisfaction. It probably would have felt even better if Tony and I weren't in such a bad place.

When I got home that night, I sat on the couch and stared at the wall. I missed Tony so much and it was driving me crazy. I decided to call him. When it rang three times, I assumed he wasn't going to answer.

I heard the click on the line. "Hey," he said quietly.

"Hi."

We were silent for a while.

"I'm sorry for calling. I just really miss you."

I heard a voice in the background. "Excuse me for a moment," he whispered. His voice sounded like it was away from the receiver.

"I'm sorry to bother you. Where are you?"

"I'm with Victoria."

"Oh."

It was silent again.

"What are you doing?" I asked.

"Are you fucking kidding me?"

"I—I'm just wondering."

"We're talking to her distributors in Milan for your company," he snapped. "What else would we be doing? Fucking? If I wanted to fuck her, I would do it."

"That isn't what I meant," I said quickly. "I really was just curious."

He sighed. "I'm sorry I snapped."

"It's okay. I deserved it."

"No you didn't," he said gently.

"Did you tell her everything?"

"No," he said. "I told her you gave me the letter, which wasn't opened."

"Oh..."

"I don't want to ruin the relationship between you. You need her, Cassie."

I wasn't expecting that.

"I told her you just forgot."

"What did you say in regards to the letter?"

He sighed loudly. "It's none of your business what I said."

"I'm sorry…"

He cursed. "I'm sorry for being such an asshole. I told her I was in love with you and I intend to marry you. That there will never be anything between she and I."

I felt my heart melt. "You intend to marry me?"

"I thought that was obvious."

I breathed a sigh of relief, glad that Victoria had been rejected.

"It hurts me that you even had to ask."

"Well, she's a fucking supermodel."

"Shut the hell up. I'm sick of hearing that."

I fell silent.

"I should go," he said. "We still have some things to do."

"Can I see you? I really miss you."

"Not tonight," he said. "I'm still livid."

"Oh…okay."

"Come by when you get off work tomorrow. I'll be better then."

"Okay," I said happily.

"Cassie, I know I'm being a jerk right now, but I want you to know that I love you with my whole heart. There's no room for anyone else but you. And I'm sorry for behaving this way."

That was music to my ears. "I love you too."

"I'll make it up to you when I see you."

"And I'll do the same."

There was a smile in his voice. "Maybe you could wear that scarf you made me…just the scarf."

I blushed. "I might…"

"Make sure you bring it over."

"I won't forget."

"Bye, baby."

"Bye."

I waited until he hung up before I put the phone down. Now I felt a million times better. He and I were going to be okay. And Victoria had no idea anything was wrong. Her evil plan hadn't worked. She might try again, but I wasn't concerned about it. I had to forget about the heartbreak I suffered from Danny. It was in the past and it needed to stay there.

There was a knock on my door. I stayed on the couch for a moment, trying to guess who might be visiting me. I knew it wasn't Tony. I walked to the peep hole and looked through. My heart raced when I recognized the face on the other side. It was Janet.

Maybe she came to apologize to me, to make everything better. Tony would get his sister back and my best friend would be returned to me. I opened the door and looked at her.

She didn't look remorseful or sad. If anything, she looked like she would rip my throat out then feed it to a pack of wild dogs. She crossed her arms over her chest and glared at me.

"Hey," I said hesitantly.

"You have a lot of fucking nerve."

"Excuse me?"

"My brother is more important to me than anything. He isn't just my family, he's my best friend. And you took him away from me."

"No, you did that, Janet."

"Shut the hell up and let me talk. I didn't get to see him on his birthday. My mom asked why we weren't doing anything and I had to lie to her. I hate lying. I didn't call

Tony on his birthday. I didn't even get him a gift. I miss him and I want him back."

"You can have him whenever you want him," I said.

She shook her head. "Layla told me you started your own clothing line. Apparently it's going really well."

Shit.

"And I know who's responsible for that. You've only been together for a few months and you're already stealing his wallet."

"It's not what you think."

"No, it's exactly what I think."

"I'm not using him! He forced me to do it."

"You're such a fucking liar."

"And I'm paying him back."

"You and I both know Tony would never take it. You took millions of dollars from him. You're a fucking lying skank."

I felt the anger explode inside me. "I love him. I don't care what you think."

"You love him?" she said with a laugh. "You have no right to say that."

"I tell him every day."

"My brother is ruining his life with you."

That stung. "I treat him right."

"By taking his mail, reading it, and then hiding it from him?"

My eyes widened. "How did you know that?"

"Scott tells me everything." She glared at me. "I can't believe you would do that to him, especially after everything he's done for you."

"I made a mistake. He and I worked it out."

"You will end this relationship with him."

"Janet, I wish things could be different. I really do. But you're falsely accusing me of using him. I'm not going to give in and neither is he. We are both really happy. You should be supportive."

"I love my brother and I'll do everything I can to protect him, even if it costs our relationship. Do you realize what you're doing to him? You're ostracizing him from his family. Do you have any idea how close we are? You're ruining that. Tony can't see his own nephew, he can't see me, and he can't see my parents when we see them. You're ruining something that means the world to him. If you really love him, you'll end the relationship."

I stared at her, feeling sick to my stomach.

"You know I'm right. He can always get a new girlfriend. But he can't get a new family."

"Janet, I swear that I'm not with him for his money."

"Your words mean nothing to me. I might believe that you love him if you let him go. It's the right thing to do."

I took a deep breath. "But I make him happy."

"No, you don't. In a year he'll realize he made a horrible mistake. He'll resent you and loathe you for it. Believe me. I know my brother." She stepped away. "I expect you to do the right thing. And if you do, you and I might be able to work on our relationship."

"Even if I did, I wouldn't want it."

She turned on her heel and left.

17

I got another huge order from a company in Milan the next day.

"Cassie, this is insane," Orlando said. "I mean, you're already a millionaire."

"Yeah."

He raised an eyebrow. "Did you hear what I said?"

"Yes, Orlando."

"You're already a fashion icon. There are too many orders that can even be filled. I bet Pia is being grilled at this very moment."

I leaned back in my chair and thought about my conversation with Janet.

"What the hell is wrong with you?" Orlando said.

"I'm just…distracted."

"Well, stop being distracted. You're fucking rich."

"No, I'm not. Everything I'm making goes back to Tony."

He rolled his eyes. "It's still exciting. You've already made back the investment you put into this company. The next time you get paid it will actually be for a profit."

"It is amazing," I said simply.

"You're living the dream, Cassie. In ten years, you'll have more money than you know what to do with."

"I don't care about money," I said.

"Then what do you care about?"

"Tony."

I'm not following," he said. "Is there something going on between you?"

I didn't want to talk about it. It's all I've been thinking about. Now that I had fallen so madly in love with him, I realized how selfish I was. I was selfish from the beginning. I was no good for him. The reason why I feared being alone was because I was meant to be alone. Danny cheated on me because I wasn't good for him either. I had to end it with him. He was losing his entire family because of me. Janet was right. I had to do the right thing.

"Everything is fine," I lied.

He eyed me. "It doesn't seem like it."

"I need to get back to work, Orlando."

"I can take the hint." He turned and walked away.

I went through my finances and determined how much money I had. A lot of dough was rolling in. With the expenses and the income, we had almost broke even. That was enough for now. I had enough credit and had a successful business so I could get a loan to pay back Tony. I could pay myself back through time.

After work I went to the bank and applied for it. I was surprised that I got it. I made some profit from the business but not a lot. The interest rate of the loan was ridiculous, but I needed to pay back Tony. I couldn't do this without returning his money to him first.

When I arrived at his apartment, I didn't want to go inside. I stood in the hallway for half an hour, dreading the moment. After I finally stilled my heart, I walked inside. Tony was sitting at the kitchen table, going through the files from the company.

He stood up and kissed me, making me melt immediately. "Baby, I missed you."

"I missed you too." I wrapped my arms around him and held him tightly. It felt so good to feel his embrace. I never wanted to let go. I could stay like that forever.

He pulled away and kissed my forehead. "How are you?"

I was worse than I had ever been. "Good. You?"

"Amazing," he said. "I can't believe how well the line is doing. You're a huge success."

"No, you are. You made all of this happen."

"But you're the one who designed the clothes."

I shrugged. "It's not that hard."

"Maybe for a genius like you." He rubbed his nose against mine. "Let's go in the bedroom."

I couldn't let that happen. If we made love, I'd chicken out. I already didn't want to do this. Being with him would just make it harder. "There's something I want to give you."

"A surprise?"

"I guess." I pulled out the box that held his scarf and put it on the table.

"Ooh," he said. "I'm glad you remembered this."

I opened my wallet and handed him the check. "Here's your money back."

He raised an eyebrow when he looked at it. "What?"

"This is all the money you invested in the company."

"But how is that possible?" He took the check and studied it. "Did you get a loan?"

"It doesn't matter. We're square."

"Cassie, the whole point of me giving you the money is so you wouldn't have to pay interest."

"I've made a lot of money already," I said. "I'll be able to pay that back in no time."

"But this was still completely unnecessary."

"It gives me peace of mind."

He stared at me. "Baby, what's wrong?"

I took a deep breath. I couldn't cry. It wasn't going to happen. "I've been thinking…"

His eyes were glued to my face.

"I don't think we should be together anymore."

His eyes immediately lost their light. "What?"

"This isn't working for me." I couldn't think of anything else to say. I was just pulling shit out of my ass. If I told him the truth, he wouldn't accept the break up.

"What are you talking about, Cassie?"

"I don't want to be with you anymore," I said firmly.

He ran his fingers through his hair. "I don't believe you."

"Well, I don't."

"What's going on?"

"We're over, Tony. I can't be in this relationship anymore. I don't feel the same way."

"Cassie, I said I was sorry for the way I behaved and I meant it. I didn't mean to be an ass to you."

I looked away.

He grabbed my hips and looked into my face. "You're just upset and I understand that. The last two days have been rough for both of us." He kissed me and my knees became weak. His hands dug into my sides and his tongue slid across mine. I felt myself give in to the love I had for him. I pulled away before it could go any further.

"No," I said.

His eyes widened. "I don't understand what's going on."

"We're over. That's it."

"But why?"

"I don't want to be with you anymore. I made that clear. Go be with Victoria."

"Where the hell is this coming from? Why are you pushing me away?"

"I'm not," I said. "I just want to break up."

"But you love me."

I kept my mouth closed.

"Cassie, you love me."

This was going nowhere.

"We aren't ending this. You can't break up with me. I won't let you."

"I just wanted the money to start the company," I said simply. "I got what I wanted. Now let me go."

He dropped his hands to his sides. He looked pained, like someone shot him in the stomach. "You're lying."

"I'm really not," I said with a straight face. "I got the investment I needed and I paid you back. My empire is ready. I don't need you anymore."

Tony stepped back, his eyes watery.

I hated the look on his face. I hated it, I hated it.

"You were using me this whole time?"

I nodded.

"But—you weren't. No one is that good of an actor."

"Well, I am."

He looked at the floor then ran his fingers through his hair. "I don't believe you."

"I'm sorry you don't. It'll just make it harder for you."

Tony blinked his eyes and stopped the tears from falling. It was torture to watch. "Well, I'm okay with that."

"What?"

"I still make you happy. I can give you everything you could ever want. Please don't go."

"I can't believe you…"

"Cassie, you're everything to me. I can't lose you."

"But I'm just using you."

He said nothing.

I couldn't believe that. I knew Tony was in love with me, but I didn't realize how much. He was totally selfless, loving me even though I was a liar. "No."

"Cassie, I just don't believe you. I refuse to believe you."

"I'm not lying."

He shook his head. "I'm not letting you go. You're too damn good to get away."

I avoided his gaze. "Goodbye, Tony." I turned toward the door.

He stood in front of it, blocking my escape. "No. We'll work on this."

"I don't want to work on it!"

"That's too fucking bad," he said. "You aren't running from a little bump in the road. And don't tell me you're using me. I know it's a fucking lie. You can't pull that shit on me."

"I'M NOT LYING!"

He stared me down, not backing down.

"Get out of my way."

"No."

I tried to get around him but he grabbed me, holding onto my arms.

"Let me go."

He carried me to the couch then pinned me down. I struggled against him but he was too strong.

"Get off me."

Tony rested his leg on my chest and pulled off his shirt.

As soon as I saw his chest, I felt alarmed. I couldn't let this happen. If it did, I'd be lost. It would make it so much harder to sever the relationship. "Stop."

He leaned over me and held me down while he got his pants off. "No. You're lying to me. When I'm inside you, you'll start thinking clearly."

"Tony, I said get off me." I tried to sit up but he held me down.

When he was naked, he lifted my dress and moved my underwear over.

"Please don't," I begged.

Tony entered me, his face pressed close to mine.

As soon as I felt him, the fight was over. I lied back and closed my eyes, a moan escaping my lips.

Tony cupped my face and kissed me gently, his lips separating mine. When I felt his tongue dance around mine, my nails dug into his back. His warm breaths filled my mouth, making me lose my train of thought. All I knew was that I loved Tony and wanted to be with him. I was lost in him, feeling the connection between us.

He thrust into me gently, feeling no resistance at all. His breaths were deep and heavy, and I felt it on my skin. When he was inside me, I felt close to him, like we were a single person. I couldn't resist him. He was the love of my life. There was no one I would rather spend the rest of my life with. Every time we made love, it was the first time. I never had a boyfriend that was my best lover and my greatest friend. Every touch was magic, explosive.

"Tony..."

He moved into me faster. "I love you, baby."

"God, I love you so much."

"I know you do." He grabbed my neck while he moved into me hard and fast. "So stop lying to me."

I gripped him while the orgasm started between my legs. It burst into flame and sent me spiraling. It was stronger than I've ever felt. I felt dizzy and lightheaded, overwhelmed with the emotion. Spending a lifetime without him would be unbearable. I didn't want to lose him. "Yeah…"

Tony bit his lip while he came inside me. I felt his cock twitch as it released, filling me. He grabbed my face and kissed me aggressively. The sweat dripped down his back and I felt it on my fingertips. It was warm and slippery. When he pulled out, I whined in pain, not wanting to feel him leave me. He broke our kiss then looked down at me, anger and desire flashing. "Don't ever pull a stunt like that again." He picked me up and carried me into his bedroom. When we were under the covers, he held onto me like I would slip away. His hands glided over my body and through my hair, treasuring every part of me.

We lay in the dark for a long time. Neither one of us spoke because there was nothing to stay. I wanted to stay here forever, never leave his arms. But I knew I had to. Our relationship had to end. I wished I hadn't slept with him, but I didn't regret it. It felt so good. I loved making love to him. There was nothing I enjoyed more.

When he fell silent, I lied still. I waited for the right moment to leave. When I heard him breathe deeply, I made my move. I slipped from under the covers toward the edge of the bed. His hand grabbed me and pulled me back.

"Do I have to tie you up?" he whispered.

I said nothing, feeling his fingers tighten around me.

"Come here."

I did as he asked. When his arms were wrapped around me, I felt my eyes grow heavy. I feel asleep and had a dreamless slumber. When I woke up the next morning, he was still asleep. And he seemed to be in a deep sleep. I left the bed and changed before I walked into the kitchen. A tear fell down my face when I placed the key to his apartment on the table. I left the scarf I made for him then walked out the door without looking back.

18

I didn't want to go to work the next day but I did. I worked on a few designs without really paying attention to what I was doing. The only thing I liked about being there was the distraction. I didn't think about Tony every second.

I kept my phone off just in case he tried to call me. When he saw the key on the table, he would know we were really over. He might chase me again, but he might give up too. I wasn't sure what I wanted him to do. I grabbed the work phone and called Janet.

"Hello?"

"It's Cassie."

"Why are you calling me?" she snapped.

"I did it."

She paused for a moment. "You broke up with my brother?"

My voice came out shaky. "Yeah…"

"You did the right thing."

It didn't feel like it. "Are you happy now?"

She sighed. "Cassie, I don't blame you for wanting the security my brother has. Any girl would want it. And I don't think you're a bad person because of it. I just didn't want that for my brother. It really wasn't personal."

"I wasn't with him for his money," I snapped. "I said that so many times now. The only reason why I ended the relationship was because he was miserable on his birthday. I know how much his family means to him. You were the one was being selfish by making him choose. And I know he would have picked me forever because you're wrong, Janet. Totally wrong about me. But I did it for him. That's it. There is no other reason."

"Well, you made the right decision. And we can be friends again."

"Janet, you're a fucking bitch. I never want to be your friend again." I slammed the phone down and hung up. When I felt the tears fall, I covered my face and let myself break down. None of this was fair. Tony shouldn't have to choose between his girlfriend and his family, especially when I did nothing wrong.

The phone rang but I didn't answer it. I took a moment to compose myself and control my voice. "Hello?" I said when I answered.

"Turn on your fucking phone."

I didn't want to deal with this right now. "Don't call me."

"You're my girlfriend. I'll call you whenever I feel like it."

"We broke up."

He hung up.

I heard the line go dead. I must have really pissed him off. But that was okay because it's exactly what I wanted. I got back to work and tried to stop thinking about Tony. Minutes later, my office door swung in. Tony stood there, looking angry and insane. He slammed the door and locked it.

"What the hell is wrong with you?" he snapped.

"What's wrong with me? You're the one who won't accept the fact that we're done."

He slammed his hand on the desk. When he pulled away, I saw his key. "This belongs to you."

"I don't want it."

"That's too fucking bad. I gave it to you."

"Why are you making this so difficult?" I yelled.

"Because you don't want to break up. I can see it in your eyes."

"Yes, I do."

"Why are you doing this?" he snapped. "Why are you pushing me away?"

"Because that's what people do when they break up!"

He came around the desk and grabbed me. "No."

"Tony, you need to leave."

He picked me up and placed me on the desk.

I knew what he was doing. "No!"

Tony held me down and pulled me to the end of the desk. "I'll do this as many times as it takes."

"Tony, stop this now!"

He pulled down his jeans then lifted up my dress. "I'll stop when I know you want me to." He pulled off my underwear then slipped inside me.

"Fuck you," I said I rolled me head back.

He rocked into me slowly. "Do you want me to stop?"

I bit my lip while I felt him.

"Tell me you want me to stop."

I grabbed his forearms and dug my nails into his skin.

Tony stopped moving.

I moaned in frustration.

"Tell me you want me to make love to you."

I said nothing.

He didn't move, just staring into my eyes.

I grabbed his hips and started to move against him. "Tony…"

"Yes?"

"Please."

He moved inside me hard and fast.

I lied back and enjoyed it. The orgasm hit as soon as I let myself go. I knew Theresa and Orlando could hear us but I didn't care. He bucked inside me when he reached the same threshold. His moaned while he made his final thrusts, coming inside me.

When he pulled out, he grabbed my face and kissed me. "You are mine."

I said nothing, still breathing heavily.

Tony pulled on his clothes while he stared me down.

"Tony, I want to break up."

"It didn't seem like it a second ago."

"We were just fucking. I would have screwed any other hot guy I saw."

"I'm having a hard time believing that."

I fixed my hair and pulled down my dress. "Tony, I mean it. We're over."

"I'll pick you up at seven."

"Are you even listening to me?"

"Yes, but I'm also ignoring you."

I glared at him. "Why won't you accept what I said? If one person wants to break up, you break up. It doesn't have to be mutual."

"I'll accept it when you give me a valid reason. Until then, I know you're pulling shit out of your ass. I think you're just scared that I'm going to hurt you so you'd rather be alone than have to deal with that possibility. We were apart for two days and it almost killed you. That's not a reason to break up. That's called fighting. All couples do it."

"You aren't listening to me," I said. "I was using you so I could build my company. Now that I have what I want, I don't need you anymore."

"You're a terrible liar." He walked to the door. "I'll see you tonight."

"Tony!"

"What?"

"I mean it. We're done."

He stared at me. "We're never done." He left my office and shut the door behind him.

I sighed in frustration. Tony was making this impossible.

When I got off work, I didn't go to my apartment. Instead, I went out for a drink with Layla.

"I broke up with him," I said.

"Are you okay?"

"No."

"Why did you do it?"

"Because he's lost his whole family," I said. "I can't let him pick me over them."

"But he's only picking because Janet made him."

"She's wrong but I can't let Tony lose everything," I said.

She shook her head. "I'm not talking to Janet anymore."

"What?"

"This is unacceptable. You two are in love and she's ruining that. It's wrong."

I shrugged. "What else am I supposed to do?"

"Not give in."

"It's not about giving in," I said. "It's about what's best for Tony. You didn't see him on his birthday. He was totally miserable."

"I'm surprised Tony accepted the break up."

"He hasn't," I said. "He keeps tracking me down and fucking my brains out, thinking that will change my mind."

"It would change mine," Layla said with a smile.

"Well, it isn't working."

"It's because he won't let Janet control his relationship."

"I didn't tell him the real reason," I said. "I said I was using him for his company."

"You did?"

"But he doesn't believe me."

"Because he knows you," she said. "You wouldn't do something like that."

"I wish Janet thought that."

"Fuck her," she snapped. "I don't care if Kyle is Scott's brother. I'm done with her."

"I don't want that," I said. "Please don't ruin your relationship because of me."

"How can I let my best friend be treated like this?" she said. "No, this bullshit has gone on long enough. "

I smiled. "Well, thank you."

"I got your back."

My phone rang and I looked at the screen. It was Tony. I ignored it. He called again. After I ignored it, he called again. I turned it off to avoid the calls altogether.

Layla smiled. "You think that's going to stop him?"

"I have to get rid of him."

"You can't," she said. "He's madly in love with you. He'll never let you go."

Layla's phone rang and she answered it. "Hey, babe." She stirred her drink while she listened. "At Tully's. Why?" She paused. "Yeah, she's here."

I narrowed my eyes in suspicion.

"Hello?" She looked at the phone. "Well, that was weird. He didn't even say bye."

I sighed. "Tony."

She smiled. "I told you he would track you down."

"I should go before he gets here."

"And go where?" she asked. "Your apartment? He'll break down the door."

"Can I stay at your place?"

"I don't want him to break down *my* door."

I sighed. "I'll figure it out." I turned to leave the table and saw Tony walk inside. "Holy shit, he's fast."

Layla looked amused. "He should be in the CIA."

When Tony saw me, his face lit up in a rage.

"Oh great," I said sarcastically.

"I think I'm going to go…"

Tony marched to me then grabbed my hip. "Why does my sister think we're broken up?" he said without preamble.

"Because we are."

He narrowed his eyes. "That's why you broke up with me. Because she's making you."

"She isn't making me," I said.

"It sounds like it."

"Tony, you are totally miserable without your family."

"I'm miserable that my sister, the person I held in the highest honor, is being a fucking bitch. That's what I'm miserable about. Breaking up with me isn't going to change that."

"I can't be the reason you lose your family…I can't."

"You aren't," he said. "Janet is."

"Tony, this isn't working. I'm sorry."

"Don't give into her. I know she's your friend—"

"She isn't my friend," I said. "And I never want to be her friend again."

"Then don't do this."

"I have to. You can always find a new girlfriend. You can't find another family."

"You are my family," he said.

My eyes softened. "Don't make this harder for me."

"No, I'm going to. This is a stupid reason to break up. It changes nothing."

"Tony, I love you. I have to do what's best for you."

"Losing you isn't what's best for me."

I averted my gaze.

"So this is it?" he asked sadly.

"Yes."

His eyes lost their light. His jaw was tense. He ran his fingers through his hair then took a deep breath, his eyes starting to turn red. "Okay."

That caught me by surprise. "Okay?"

"You told me the real reason. If that's what you want, I have to accept it." He didn't look at me.

I wasn't expecting him to give up.

"Goodbye, Cassie." He turned around and left, leaving me standing in the bar alone.

19

This was the hardest breakup I'd ever endured. Even when Danny cheated on me, it was nothing compared to this. I couldn't sleep, I couldn't eat, I couldn't move. I went to work but hardly got anything done. Orlando and Theresa were sympathetic and gave me space. I didn't speak to anyone because I didn't have anything to say.

Tony hadn't contact me in any way. A part of me hoped he would break down my door and take me on my kitchen table, saying he would never let me go. I never hated anyone in my life, but I was starting to hate Janet. Tony was the best thing that ever happened to me. I lost him due to no fault of my own.

The days went by but it didn't get better. I almost called him a few times but I stayed strong and didn't make the call. I wondered what he was doing. I wondered if he was seeing anyone. The thought made me sick to my stomach. It was hard to sleep in my bed because it still smelled like him. Instead of bringing me comfort, it brought me tears. I would wash them but I was afraid to let him go. I wasn't ready to.

Layla came over and comforted me as much as she could. Kyle was there too. They were the only friends I had that understood my pain. We never spoke about Tony, and Janet was never mentioned. There was a huge elephant in the room that no one addressed.

Tony still did work for my company but everything was relayed through Victoria. She comforted me about the breakup. I knew she wanted him but she seemed genuinely sympathetic. Perhaps it was because Tony had rejected her completely.

I took a cab by his building on the way to work and on the way home. I hoped I would get a glimpse of him on the sidewalk or getting into a cab. It was pathetic but I missed him so much. I would do anything just to hold him again.

That weekend, I stayed home and did nothing. I hadn't been grocery shopping in a long time. I had lost so much weight that I really could be a model if I wanted to. My clothes didn't fit anymore. They were baggy and unflattering. I felt weak all the time. The only comfort I had was knowing Tony had his family back. His sister was his closest friend. I knew he couldn't live without her.

When there was a knock on the door, I didn't know what to do. No one visited me. I didn't have any friends at the moment. I had been shutting everyone out. I wondered if I ordered a pizza but just forgot about it.

When I reached the peephole, I saw Janet on the other side. I stilled when I recognized her. I had no idea what she wanted. I opened the door and stared at her.

"I broke up with him. I did as you asked," I said. "So if you came here to harass me, go fuck yourself."

She averted her gaze, seeming frightened and on the verge of tears. "Can I talk to you for a second?"

"No."

"Please."

"I've never been miserable in my entire life. And that's all because of you. I don't owe you anything. Get the fuck away from me."

"It's about Tony."

"Is he okay?" I blurted. "What's wrong?"

"Can I come in?"

"No. You aren't welcome here. Now tell me about him."

"He—he won't talk to me," she said. "He has a restraining order against me. He's isolated himself from my sister and my parents. He wants nothing to do with us."

I didn't know what to say to that. I broke up with him so he'd have his family back. If he was ignoring them, why didn't he just come back to me?"

"Layla told me you slept with him before you even knew he had money," she said. "And I saw the check you wrote him on the kitchen table."

"What's your point?"

"I—I know you weren't using him."

"I've been saying that this entire time."

"I'm sorry I didn't believe you," she whispered.

That didn't mean anything to me. "If that's why you came here, you can go."

"I need your help," she said with a trembling lip.

"I'm not going to do anything for you."

"Please listen to me." A tear fell down her cheek. "Tony said he wants nothing to do with me. He'll only make an exception if you and I become friends again and I get you to take him back. If I don't do that, I'll never see him again."

"He said that?"

She nodded.

I felt my heart start to beat again. He still wanted me. He still loved me.

"Please get back together with my brother. Please."

"You don't need to beg me," I said. "I want him for the rest of my life."

"Then please accept my apology and be my friend again."

"That I can't do…"

She wiped her tears away. "I'll do anything, Cassie."

"I can't just forget what you did to me. Stuff like that doesn't just happen overnight."

"Cassie, I was a total and complete bitch. I know I was. I regret everything I said and everything I did. I was so convinced that you wanted to hurt my brother that I went overboard. I was out of my mind. When it comes to my family, I can't see straight. You know that better than anyone."

I crossed my arms over my chest.

"Cassie, please just consider it."

"That's all I can give you."

She nodded. "Thank you."

I walked inside and grabbed my purse.

"Where are you going?" she asked.

"To get my boyfriend back."

"I'll come with you."

"We'll probably be taking each other's clothes off. You might not want to do that," I said.

"I just want to talk to him."

"I can't guarantee that he will."

"I have to try," she said.

We left my apartment and walked to his, neither one of us speaking. When I got to his floor, I ran to his door then banged my fists, unable to wait until he answered it. When he did, his eyes looked dark and sad. He looked thin, like he hadn't been eating. And his hair was messy. He took a deep breath when he saw me.

The tears fell before I could even stop them. I jumped into his arms and held him as tight as I could. His arms wrapped around me and he sniffed, letting the emotion overcome him.

"I'm so glad you're back," he whispered.

I pulled away and kissed him. "Why didn't you come get me?"

"You said I had to get my family back first. So that's what I did. I gave Janet the same ultimatum she gave me. I'm glad it worked."

I kissed his tears away and pressed my face close to his. "I'm sorry about everything. I should have just listened to you."

"We're together now. It doesn't matter anymore."

I closed my eyes and held onto him.

"Tony?" Janet asked.

He pulled away and looked at her. "What?"

"I held my end of the deal."

Tony turned to me. "Do you forgive her?"

Janet took a deep breath and stared at me, silently begging me with her eyes. I shouldn't forgive Janet for what she did to me, even if she had good intentions, but I had to do what was best for Tony. "Yes."

Janet released the air in her lungs.

"I want to see you apologize to her," Tony said. "And our relationship will never be the same. You have to earn my trust and friendship before we can put ourselves back together."

She nodded. "Cassie, I'm sorry I put you through this. It was wrong. I was totally wrong about you."

"It's okay," I said.

Tony looked at his sister. "You're lucky Cassie is such a compassionate person."

"I know I am," she said. "I hope I can get my best friend back one day."

I didn't respond.

Tony placed his arm around my waist then rubbed his nose against mine. "We'll talk to you later, Janet."

"Okay," she said. "Can we get lunch tomorrow?"

Tony looked at her.

"All of us?'

"Cassie and I are going to be busy this week."

"Oh…"

"But we'll do something next week."

She smiled. "Okay. I'll see you later." She left the apartment and closed the door behind her.

Tony turned back to me. "I'm sorry about everything."

"I'm sorry too."

"So, we're both sorry?" he asked with a smile.

"I shouldn't have given in to Janet."

"No, you were right. Everything worked out in the end. Now I got my sister back, you got your friend back, and everything is okay."

I sniffed and wiped my tears away. "It's been hell without you."

"Believe me. I know."

I pressed my face against his chest and held it there.

"Move in with me."

I felt my heart stop. "What?" I asked as I pulled away.

"Move in with me," he repeated. "You're the one. I know you are."

"Are you sure?"

He smiled at me. "I can tell that your answer is yes just by looking into your eyes."

I wiped my tears away. "I would love to live with you."

He pulled me to his chest. "And I don't care if my sister objects."

"I'll slap her if she does."

He chuckled. "I don't think she will. She knows she was wrong. And I know she'll regret it for the rest of her life. This doesn't justify what she did, but she was trying to protect me."

"I know…"

"I'm glad you're willing to forgive her. That must be hard for you."

"It was," I said. "But I would do anything for you."

He grabbed my hips and pressed his face close to mine. "Let's go in the bedroom."

"And not come out for a week."

"Or ever."

The story continues….

Viola

(Book Six in the Alpha Series)

Available Soon

About the Author

E. L. Todd was raised in California where she attended California State University, Stanislaus and received her bachelor's degree in biological sciences, then continued onto her master's degree in education. While she considers science to be interesting, her true passion is writing. She works as an assistant editor at Final-Edits.com.

By E. L. Todd

Soul Catcher

(Book One of the Soul Saga)

Soul Binder

(Book Two of the Soul Saga)

Soul Relenter

(Book Three of the Soul Saga)

Only For You

(Book One of the Forever and Always Series)

Forever and Always

(Book Two of the Forever and Always Series)

Edge of Love

(Book Three of the Forever and Always Series)

Force of Love

(Book Four in the Forever and Always Series)

Fight for Love

(Book Five in the Forever and Always Series)

Lover's Roulette

(Book Six in the Forever and Always Series)

Happily Ever After

(Book Seven of the Forever and Always Series)

Sadie

(Book One of the Alpha Series

Elisa

(Book Two of the Alpha Series)

Connected by the Sea

(Book One of the Hawaiian Crush Series)

Breaking Through the Waves

(Book Two of the Hawaiian Crush Series)

Connected by the Tide

(Book Three of the Hawaiian Crush Series)

Taking the Plunge

(Book Four of the Hawaiian Crush Series)